THE CRAFTY COACH

ZAC MARKS

"Some people think football is a matter of life and death. I assure you, it's much more serious than that."

Bill Shankly

1. FULL-TIME?

'You're never gonna play football again.'

I didn't see it coming. There was no warning. None.

Sometimes you get news so bad that you can't take it in. It doesn't seem real.

I sit on the grass with the rest of the team, looking at the coach. He can't be serious?

I'd rather be told that I'll never eat chocolate again or we can't afford a TV any more. I'm not one of those kids who plays at the weekend for something to do. Football is my life.

But it's over.

'You're never gonna play football again.'

Ok, that's not what our coach says. Those aren't his actual words. It's just how it sounds as he explains he has to move away for work and no-one else has stepped up to coach us. We can play our game on Saturday, but after that, it's finished. The Ferndale Foxes will fold.

'I'm sorry, lads, I really am.' Darren looks guilty. He set up the Foxes, and he's been a brilliant coach. I remember how excited I was when I found out that someone was putting together a team in our village. I signed up straight away and never missed a practice or match. Darren has been there through thick and thin, coaching us in the freezing cold, the wind and the rain. I'd do anything for him.

Why is he only telling us now?

He seems to know what I'm thinking. 'I was going to say something sooner, but I kept hoping one of the other parents would step up. I didn't want to worry you. I've loved being your coach - it's been amazing. We play against Waterford on Saturday. That's our last game together, so let's make it a good one, yeah?'

I try to smile, to wish Darren good luck in his new job, to tell him it isn't his fault, but I can't. Some of the lads manage it, and I'm glad. After the years he's put in coaching us, he deserves it.

But I'm too angry.

I'm like that: my passion gets the better of me.

Ask any referee.

A few minutes later, Dave and I walk over to the car park. He's as gutted as I am.

'What are we gonna do?' he asks, like he expects me to solve the problem.

'There's nothing we can do!' I spit back, furious. 'You

heard him. It's over.'

'We could always play for a different team?'

'Like where? The nearest team is in Welbeck and that's a mission away. And I'm not playing for *them*.'

Dave knows what I mean. He doesn't want to play there either. It's hardly a great option. There are no good teams around here.

Dave's mum is waiting by the car. 'How was training?' she asks.

Dave shrugs and gets in.

'That good, huh?' says his mum. She probably thinks that Dave is sulking because he missed a penalty or something. 'Do you need a lift, Jed?'

'No thanks, I'll walk.'

She already takes me to the away games. I can't expect her to drop me home after training as well. Besides, I need time to think.

It's a ten-minute walk from the pitch to my place. Half-way there, I pull my boots off. They're a size too small and they hurt. I haven't told my mum because she's under enough pressure as it is. She works two jobs just to pay the bills.

I pad up the street to my house. Truth be told, it's a right dump. It always has been, ever since we got the keys off the council. There's a rusty fridge in the front yard and weeds grow between the paving slabs. The paintwork on the windows is cracked and peeling. I never invite my friends around because I'm too embarrassed.

It's not mum's fault. Dad's really the one to blame: he left when I was a baby. I can't even remember what he looks like.

I hunt around in my bag for my key and slip it in the lock. I step onto bare floorboards and junk mail. I should pick it up, but I just kick it aside and crash onto the sofa with a deep sigh. The tears roll down my cheeks as the terrible news sinks in.

No more football.

No more Foxes.

It can't be happening. It just can't.

I lie there, sprawled out on the settee in my blue-and-white training kit, trying to come up with a plan - *any* plan - to save the team.

It's impossible. My mum hates sport and doesn't have any spare time: she'd never coach us. And Darren asked all the parents already. He said he'd laid it on pretty thick, but the other lads' parents had refused point blank. They're busy people.

Other clubs are miles away, and mum doesn't have a car. I can't expect someone else's parents to always give me a lift.

There's no way to solve it. Our village is about to get even more boring than it already is. Once we've played our last match on Saturday, the only place I'll get to play football is at school. I can't imagine what that's going to feel like.

My phone buzzes on the coffee table. I pick it up and glance at the cracked screen. It's Dave.

'What?' I say. I don't like chatting on the phone, even to my best mate.

'Jed, cheer up. I've had an idea!'

Dave's a natural optimist, not like me. One time, we got creamed by the worst team in the league. The final score was 7-1 and Dave still came off the pitch smiling.

'What are you so cheerful about?' I asked him.

'I scored, didn't I?' he replied.

It's that kind of sunny optimism that makes me want to punch him.

So, when I hear his words over the phone, I can't allow him to get my hopes up. Whatever he's planning won't work. But I guess I might as well hear him out.

'Yeah?' I say, gruffly. 'What's this great idea?'

'Well, the other day I was round Rex's house, right? He had a new game and asked me over.'

'Sure. Thanks for the invite.'

Dave ignores me and presses on. 'While I'm there, this

argument blows up between Rex's brother Sammo and his mum. Sammo's passed his driving test, but his mum won't let him drive her car unless he pays for petrol and insurance and everything.'

'And?'

'Well, she tells Sammo that if he wants to drive the car, then he has to get himself a part-time job. But Sammo says there aren't any jobs going in the village.'

'Is there a point to all this?' I ask. I don't deserve a friend like Dave. Not when I'm in one of my moods. 'Wait a minute, you're not suggesting we pay Sammo to be our coach, are you?'

'Yes! Sammo's amazing at football. Well, he used to be! There are pictures all over the house. He had trials and played for an academy and everything. And he's even doing a college course on sport and stuff, so he's proper qualified. He needs money, and we need a coach!'

'Right.' Dave's plan has one major drawback which I need to point out. 'And how are we gonna pay him? You planning to rob a bank?'

'Nah, we'd all stump up a few quid a week. I reckon we'd need him for two practices and one match, so let's say five hours, right? Well, if we paid him a decent rate, like eight pounds an hour, then that comes to forty pounds each week. Split that between all of us and it only costs around four quid each.'

I look around me at the ripped armchair, the cracked mirror, the ancient TV. Dave lives in a different world.

'What do you think?' he asks, waiting for a round of applause.

'I think I don't have that kind of money. If I did, then I'd be up for it. But I can't afford it.'

It's Dave's turn to go quiet. He's kicking himself. He knows I'm poor but doesn't get what that means. Why would he? He's never had to live off toast and baked beans.

'Don't worry, Jed, we can cover your share,' he offers. 'The other lads won't mind.'

'I'm not a charity case.'

I wonder if I've squashed his enthusiasm.

No chance.

'Wait up! You can get a paper round! There's one being advertised at the shop! That would pay enough!'

I groan. I don't want to get up at stupid a.m. to bike for miles around the village.

'Alfie's brother used to do that round,' I say. 'He said it's mental. It's not worth it.'

'Even to save the Foxes?'

I pause for a moment, fiddling with the badge on my shirt. I'd do anything for the team and he knows it. 'If I was up for it, do you think Sammo would coach us? For real?'

'There's one way to find out,' says Dave. 'What are you up to right now?'

'This minute? Not a lot.'

'Well, get your bike and meet me at Rex's house. We'll ask Sammo, see if he's interested. Can't hurt, can it?'

'I guess not,' I say. 'I'm on my way.'

2. SAMMO

That's how we end up riding to Rex's place. Dave's already showered and changed, but I'm still in my kit.

'Have you checked this out with Rex?' I ask, as we freewheel down the hill.

'Yeah, he's not too keen,' admits Dave. 'He says his brother's an idiot, but he can't see any better options.'

Rex lives in the posh part of the village. We push our bikes up the drive and Dave knocks. I've not been here before and I'm hoping that Rex answers the door. Instead, we're greeted by his dad.

'Ah, Dave, Jed, good of you to pop round,' he says. 'Fresh from training, I see. I hear there's a big game this weekend?'

'Yeah, sure,' agrees Dave. 'Should be a good one. Can we go up and see Rex?'

'Go right ahead.'

At the top of the stairs, a 'KEEP OUT' sign hangs on a bedroom door.

'That's Sammo's room,' whispers Dave. The door

opposite has a large gold medal hanging on it. 'Rex is in here.'

He knocks and Rex yanks it open.

'Hi guys, come in.'

There's sports equipment everywhere: tennis racquets, a cricket bat, a hockey stick, two footballs and a basketball. It's like a sports superstore. The walls are even more impressive: shelves full of trophies and framed certificates. He's got more awards than most people get in their lifetime.

'Guys,' whispers Rex, shutting the door behind us, 'are you sure you want to do this? I have to warn you: my brother is not a nice guy.'

'You're just saying that cause he's your brother,' says Dave. 'I'd say the same thing about my sister.'

'I'm not sure...' Rex trails off, worried.

Dave won't be put off. Once he's got a plan, nothing will knock him off course. 'Your brother is pretty good at football, right?'

'Sure. He's probably the best in the village.'

'And he's desperate for cash?'

'Yeah, there is that.' Rex looks uncomfortable, shifting from one foot to the other.

'So let's try it,' says Dave. 'What have we got to lose?'

Rex opens his mouth to say something, but holds

back. Instead, he nods. 'Ok, but don't say I didn't warn you.'

We shuffle across the landing. Rex knocks loudly on Sammo's door.

'WHAT?'

'It's Rex. I need to ask you something.'

The door flies open and Sammo peers out. He has a thin, pinched face and his hair hangs down stylishly over one eye. His eyes narrow as he sees the three of us standing there. 'What do you want, squirt? Make it quick.'

Dave is the only one brave enough to speak. 'We want to ask if you'll coach us. At football.'

'Why would I do that?' asks Sammo. 'I'm a busy person.'

'Because we'd pay you.'

A glimmer of interest appears in Sammo's eyes. 'How much?'

'Forty quid a week. For two practices and a game.'

Sammo smirks at us. 'You must be desperate.'

'We are,' I blurt out. 'You're our only hope.'

There's a brief silence. Either Sammo is thinking about our offer or he's working out the best way to cause us pain. I'm not sure which.

Eventually, he smiles. It's not a reassuring smile, though. More of a wicked grin. 'Ok, clean my car.'

'What?' Dave is as confused as I am. He doesn't understand.

'If you're desperate for a coach, then clean my car. Then, I'll think about your offer. If you don't, I'll just say no.'

'Seriously?' I can't believe what I'm hearing.

'Deadly,' replies Sammo. 'No shoddy work, either. Then we'll talk.'

***

Sammo's car is filthy.

I don't mean dirty, like my mum's. I mean *filthy*, like it's been dragged on its side through a pigsty. He must have been riding it off-road for laughs: mud is splattered all over the sides and the back.

Rex fetches some sponges and buckets of soapy water. We start scrubbing, trying to dislodge the muck. It's going to take ages.

'I warned you,' says Rex. 'Sammo is harsh. If he's our coach, he'll destroy us.'

'It's ok,' shrugs Dave. 'Once he's made his decision, it'll be fine.'

I'm not so sure.

The sun goes down as we work, and my hands are wet

and cold. Cleaning cars can be fun when you're in the mood, but I'm already tired from the football training and a long day at school. I need an extra hour's hard labour like I need a punch in the gut.

We've just about finished when Sammo heads outside to inspect our work.

'Well?' asks Rex, wiping a last speck of dirt off the bonnet.

'I guess the outside is ok,' says Sammo. 'I'd make a start on the inside if I were you.'

'The inside?' My heart sinks.

'If I'm gonna be your coach, you're gonna have to do what I say, Jeddy boy.' He ruffles my hair as if we're mates. 'Get used to it. I don't want any complaints or backchat.'

'But you *will* be our coach?' says Dave, keen to seal the deal, 'if we do the inside as well?'

'Maybe.' Sammo unlocks the car and disappears back inside the house.

You wouldn't think the inside of a car could be as dirty as the outside, but you'd be wrong. It seems the entire rugby team has been in here, leaving dirt on the seats and the floor. Fast food wrappers are strewn around the footwells.

'Let's get this straight,' I say to the others as I pick a slimy ketchup sachet off the mat. 'If he's our coach, then from now on we're basically his slaves?'

Rex nods, a glum look on his face. 'Now you're getting it. Imagine how I feel. I have to live with him.'

'We don't have a choice,' points out Dave. 'We need a coach.'

He's right. But that doesn't mean I have to like it.

It's dark by the time we finish. Sammo uses the light on his phone to check we've done a good job.

'It'll do,' he says, unimpressed.

'So, are you gonna be our coach?' I ask.

'Tell you what. I'll come to your game on Saturday and I'll meet with you afterwards and let you know.'

'Great! Thanks!' Dave is as enthusiastic as ever.

'Don't thank me yet,' warns Sammo. 'Wait until Saturday, and then we'll see. You boys get yourselves home. Rex, mum says you have to come in for dinner.'

Dave and I head off on our bikes.

'What did he mean by that?' I wonder.

'By what?' asks Dave.

'That we might not thank him on Saturday.'

'I dunno. Probably nothing. Stop worrying! We've saved the Foxes, Jed! We have a coach!'

Yeah, but at what cost?

3. BRIGHT

The next day, I decide to ask about the paper round. Whatever happens, I'm not gonna let the other guys pay my share of Sammo's fee.

Besides, I've worked out that if I save up the extra money each week, then I might be able to get myself some new football boots. That's got to be a win.

Outside the newsagent window is the sign: 'Paper boy/girl wanted. Age 13+. Ask inside for details.'

I've never read the small print before. I'm not thirteen for months and didn't know there was an age limit. But I need this round. I can't let a small thing like that stop me.

I take a deep breath and step inside.

'Can I help you?' The shopkeeper doesn't sound too friendly. He's not keen on schoolkids.

'I-I-I'm here about the paper round,' I say, 'if it's still available?'

The man examines me closely. No kids in the village have shown any interest for over a month. He's getting desperate to fill the role. But I'm pretty small for my age and he's suspicious.

'How old are you?' he asks.

'Thirteen,' I lie.

'You don't look it.'

'People always say that.'

'You reckon you'll be able to handle a heavy bag of papers?'

'Easy,' I assure him. 'I play loads of sports.'

'And the early mornings? You'd start at seven-fifteen, Monday to Friday.'

'Sure, no problem.' Until now, I haven't thought about the time I'll need to get up. That's gonna hurt.

'You got a bike? It's a long route.'

'Yep.'

'You realise these papers still need delivering in the rain?' He raises his eyebrows as if daring me to object.

'Like I say, I play a lot of sports. I don't mind the rain. What's the pay?'

'Fifteen pounds a week, if you're prompt and reliable.'

'I am.' That's not true either, but I need to make this happen.

The man rummages behind the counter and pulls out a tatty piece of paper. 'Get this form filled out by your mum and bring it back to me. I'm assuming your parents know you're asking about this?'

'Yeah, my mum keeps nagging me to apply for it.' I'm making this up as I go along. 'When do I start?'

'Tomorrow morning if you bring the form.'

'I will. Thanks.'

As I turn to leave, the man calls after me. 'Seven-fifteen! Don't be late!'

So, now I have another adult who gets to boss me around. But at least I got the job. Soon I'll be able to afford some new boots, and we'll have a coach for the Foxes. Things are looking up.

***

'How was school?' asks mum, as I kick off my worn black trainers. She gives me a quick hug and kiss before returning to the laundry.

'Alright. Usual.' I'm glad to see she's in a good mood as I drop onto the sofa. I decide to plunge straight in. 'Mum, the village shop needs a paper boy. I want to do it.'

'Really?' Mum looks up at me in surprise. 'Doesn't that involve getting up early?'

'Yeah, but I can do that.'

'I dunno. It'll still be dark, Jed. The roads could be dangerous.'

'I'll wear my helmet, and bright clothing, and they give

you this reflective bag with the papers in.'

'What bright clothing?' she asks. 'Everything you own is black, grey or dark blue. The only bright thing you own is this!' She pulls my orange football shirt out of the pile. 'And you can't wear your Foxes kit because you need it for matches.'

'But if I could find something bright, then you'd let me do it?'

'I can't see why not. It would be good for you to have a job. But you have to stay safe, so it has to be super-bright. Like high-viz or fluorescent or whatever.'

I leap up and give her a hug. 'By the way, I need you to sign this form, to give permission.' I hold out the crumpled piece of paper.

'You show me what you're gonna wear. Then I'll sign the form, *if* it's bright enough.'

'Deal.'

I run upstairs and throw open my wardrobe, rummaging around for anything that might work. There's a red t-shirt and a plain blue sweatshirt, both lighter than stuff I usually wear. But they're hardly going to glow in the dark.

You can't wear your football kit... As my mum's words echo in my head, I have an amazing idea. There's one person who can help me. I know someone who has a stupid number of bright clothes.

'Mum, I'm just popping to Brandon's. I'll be back in a bit.'

***

Brandon is rich. His house is like a fairytale mansion. Don't get me wrong: his parents aren't celebrities or anything. There's no Ferrari in the driveway. But they have more money than I can ever dream of.

I ring the bell, which sets off an annoying tune inside. Brandon's mum answers. She's immaculate, as always.

'Jed, how lovely to see you.' She wrinkles up her nose as she says it. They'd prefer it if their little angel didn't hang around with a filthy council-estate urchin like me. But we all have to pretend.

'Is Brandon in?'

'Yes, come in. Do you mind taking your shoes off?'

She'd probably like me to shower as well, but she holds back. I'm sure she thinks it's my fault that Brandon hates to wash. I slip off my dirty trainers, embarrassed about how grubby my white socks look against the cream carpet.

'I think Brandon is in his room,' she says. 'You know where it is.'

'Thanks.' I race upstairs and knock on Brandon's door.

'Yeah?'

As I walk in, Brandon is lying on his kingsize bed, playing on his phone. He's wearing the very latest Liverpool strip. I mean, all of it: shirt, shorts, socks. Brandon has a weird obsession with football kits, so it doesn't come as a surprise. He sits up.

'Jed! What are you doing here?'

'I need your help.' I'm straight to the point. We've played together for years. We have the sort of friendship that doesn't require small talk.

'Course. What's up?'

'You know I hate begging, but I have to borrow some old kits from you. Has Dave told you about the plan?'

'Yeah,' nods Brandon. 'It's a great idea.'

Is it, though?

I don't let my own worries ruin the moment. 'If I'm going to pay my share, then I need a paper round, and my mum won't let me do it unless I wear something bright.'

Brandon smiles. 'How bright are we talking?'

'Pretty much glow-in-the-dark.'

'Well, you've come to the right place!' He jumps off the bed and slides open his wardrobe. Even though I've seen inside before, I can't help but be impressed: he owns *so* many clothes, almost all of them football kits. It's packed from floor to ceiling.

Brandon's not loyal to any team. He loves them all. He has the strips of most Premier League clubs, as well as stuff from sides that no-one's even heard of. There are training kits, goalkeeper strips, retro shirts in every colour and combination. His parents hate him wearing football gear all the time, and occasionally they force him into something more acceptable, but he usually gets away with it.

'I have a few old kits that mum's planning to take to the charity shop. I think they'd be perfect for you. You could keep them. Let's see...' He reaches down and pulls a neon green Liverpool shirt off the shelf. 'This was their third kit a few years ago. It doesn't fit me now, and I didn't wear it that much.'

'Wow.' The shirt looks brand new. I don't like Liverpool, but it would make me visible. I can't complain.

'You should try it on.'

I drag it over my school shirt.

'See, it's perfect for you,' smiles Brandon. 'Hold on, I've got the rest of the kit here.' He throws some shorts and socks at me.

'I don't think I need the *whole* kit.'

'Mate, you said you wanted to be as bright as possible. Well, that's as bright as you're gonna get. And wait a minute, I've got another one... this one's even better!'

He pulls out another top. You need sunglasses to look at it. It's fluorescent yellow with black stripes, and so are the shorts and socks. It seems that all of Brandon's kits come as a set.

'This one's not even Premier League,' explains Brandon. 'I got it for football training but I don't play in goal so I never used it. There's some padding in the arms and legs if you have to dive. Could be useful if you come off your bike?'

'It's definitely bright enough.' It's actually horrific. I'm not sure I'll be brave enough to wear it while cycling around the village. But Brandon is being helpful and beggars can't be choosers. 'Are you sure it's ok for me to take these? Won't your mum mind?'

Brandon laughs. 'My mum would *pay* you to get rid of these. She hates them. Besides, I'm never going to use them again. They're too small. Should fit a skinny kid like you, though.'

'Cheers. You, err, don't have any bright trackies or anything do you?' I ask hopefully.

'You know me, Jed. I only wear shorts. And base layers if it's cold. You can have a pair of those. I have loads.' He throws some light grey tights in my direction. 'And I might have an old top unless mum already got rid of it...'

He dives back into his wardrobe. He emerges with a

drill top that is, as fate would have it, bright pink. It does at least have a top-brand logo across the front, which gives it more credibility than it deserves. Still, I'd need to be freezing before I wore it.

'Right, I think you're all set.'

I gather up the fluorescent pile. Yesterday he'd never have been able to persuade me to wear any of this. Today, I need it, and I'm grateful. 'Brandon, this is amazing. Thank you so much!'

'Nah, don't worry about it. What are friends for?' he says, a mischievous look on this face. 'Besides, it'll be worth it to see you in a Liverpool strip!'

I smile back. 'Shut your face. Sacrifices need to be made.'

4. EARLY

My alarm goes off at 7am. I groan and roll over, in need of more sleep. It's not an option. If I'm late on my first day, it won't end well. I force myself out of bed.

When I got home from Brandon's last night, I tried on both kits. They're a good fit: too big, if anything. As a Man City fan, I can't bear the thought of wearing a Liverpool shirt in public, but it's less embarrassing than the luminous yellow goalie outfit.

'Sorry guys,' I murmur to the City players watching me from the poster on my wall, as I pull on the neon green top. All my trackies are dark, so I reluctantly tug on the shorts and socks. Might as well make a point, I guess. I don't pull the socks up like Brandon would, just leave them bunched around my ankles. I look stupid, but mum can hardly say it isn't bright enough.

She's already up, waiting for me in the kitchen. She laughs when she sees what I'm wearing. 'Ha, I should have known you'd end up in a football kit! Are you planning to wear that every day? Shorts and socks as well?'

'Yeah, probably.' I smile back. 'Brandon gave me another one too. That's even brighter.'

'There's no "probably" here Jed. I need to know for sure.' Mum looks me in the eye. 'If you promise me you're always going to dress like that, then I'll sign your form. No slipping back into dark tracksuits and black hoodies in a few days. You need to be safe, and no driver is gonna miss you in that!'

'I might be cold in winter,' I point out, hoping she'll back down.

'Well, wear your dark stuff under it, if you like. And once you've earned enough money, you can buy yourself a bright coat or something.'

She knows me too well. I was hoping to ease off the neon kits once she'd gotten used to the idea of the paper round. Looks like that's not going to be possible. 'Ok,' I sigh. 'I'll wear it every day. I promise.'

'Then we have a deal. Where's the form?'

I fetch it and place it on the table in front of her. I've already filled out the details in pencil. She doesn't even attempt to read it, just signs on the dotted line.

'Good luck, kiddo.'

'Thanks.'

I head out the back door and alter my date of birth, so it reads like I'm thirteen. Then I grab my bike and set off.

To be fair, I can see what mum means: it's pretty dark out. Even as the first signs of dawn appear, a large black cloud looms overhead.

Please don't rain, I think to myself. Then I realise that some days that's going to happen. At some point, I'll get soaked. It's not a cheerful thought.

I arrive at the newsagents at 7.12am. He's pleased to see me. 'Have you got the form?'

'Yep,' I say, thrusting it towards him. 'It's right here.'

He glances over it, satisfied. He grabs an enormous reflective orange bag from behind the counter. 'Your papers are over there.' He points to a neat pile on a shelf. 'The house numbers and street names are written at the top. Do you know where all those are?'

I walk over and check them out. I've lived here all my life; there's only one that I'm not sure of. 'Briar's Farm? Isn't that some way out the village?'

'On the outskirts,' he admits. 'Up the farm track as you cross the bridge. Is that a problem?'

'No, no problem. Just checking I got the right place.' I don't want him to have second thoughts about giving me the job.

But Briar's Farm is an absolute mission away.

***

Most of the round is fine. The first five houses are nearby, and a few others are only a short bike ride. A couple of papers are further out, on the edges of the village. By the time I've delivered them, I've had enough. But I know what's coming: I have to ride to the farm.

The wind picks up as I reach the open road. Even though I'm pedalling like crazy, I shiver. I should have worn the base layers.

Briar's Farm is just as far as I thought: two miles at least. After what feels like an age, I skid around the corner and start up a track towards the farmhouse. The ground is boggy though it hasn't rained for days. I don't want to think about what it's like when it has. This must be why Alfie's brother quit.

The track goes on and on and the farmhouse doesn't seem to get any closer. I push on. I'm used to tough bike rides. You have to be when your family don't own a car.

Eventually, I reach a large metal gate that leads into the farmyard. I lean my bike against the fence and jog towards the house with the paper. I'm about half-way when there's a loud bark. A dog appears out of nowhere, racing towards me. I'm on its patch, and it doesn't seem friendly. I gulp and think about making a run for it, but it's already too late.

'Shep, stop that! Here boy!' The farmer walks around the corner. The dog calms down and runs to its master's side.

I realise how stupid I must look out here in my bright green football kit, but the farmer smiles.

'Morning lad. You must be the new paper boy.'

'Yeah,' I reply, shivering in the wind and wondering if I appear as scared as I feel.

'I'm Reg. Don't worry about Shep here. He won't hurt you. He just doesn't like Liverpool supporters. I can't really blame him.' The farmer grins at his own joke. 'Are you a big fan?'

'No,' I admit. 'I like Man City. But I needed something bright, for the dark roads. A mate gave me this.'

'Ah, well, we're grateful that you've taken on the round. We haven't been able to have papers delivered for over a month now. You won't give up like the last kid, will you? He didn't last long.'

'I can't,' I say. 'I need the money.'

'I'll be seeing you then.'

As I cycle back along the muddy track, I think about how much easier life would be if I were rich. But there's no point dwelling on it. I'm not. This is how my mornings are going to be from now on.

I suppose I better get used to it.

5. PAY-RISE

Saturday. 11am.

All the players are in position. We're dressed in our scruffy orange kit. The opposition—Waterford—are spotless in their top-brand red and white. They seem like a professional outfit, and I'm worried.

The referee glances around, making sure everyone is ready.

Our pitch is an embarrassment. It's just a muddy field with more dirt than grass. Whenever it rains, the whole thing becomes a swamp. The other team are far from impressed.

I lean down and tug my socks over my knees. It's the end of an era. It's the last game with Darren as our coach. We owe him a win. Surely, we can give him that?

As I scan the spectators, I notice Sammo standing on the sideline, chewing gum, his arms folded. He's wearing a tracksuit and seems keen. He could pass as a serious football coach. That's a good sign. Maybe Dave's crazy plan is going to work.

We kick off.

Everything happens fast. Whatever you say about the Foxes, we're never slow to get going. Brandon takes the centre and plays it straight to Dave. They pass back and forth a few times before sending it to Rex, on the wing.

Rex is like lightning—a streak of orange as he sprints forward. A defender tries to tackle him but Rex flicks it past and carries on. He makes it look easy.

I'm running into the box as Rex puts in a cross. I strike it towards the net, but one of the Waterford defenders gets in the way. The ball bounces off him, and he boots it down the pitch.

A goal within a minute of kick-off was probably asking too much, even for the Foxes. We'll just have to pace ourselves. I track back to support the midfield.

It's not long before we get a second chance. Dave slips by the opposition and passes to me. I turn and start up the pitch. A defender is blocking my path, but I wrong-foot him, sneaking the ball past.

I'm through. Now it's just the keeper. I dummy a shot, making him dive to the wrong side.

GOAL!

It's 1-0 to the Foxes!

Rex grabs hold of me, his face a picture of pure joy. He pulls me into a playful headlock. 'Yes, Jed!' he shouts.

'Let's have more of those!'

Brandon ruffles my hair. 'Great shot, Jed!'

'Thanks,' I grin. There's no better feeling than scoring a goal. You either get that or you don't.

It's not long before we get another break. Rex is dancing with the ball, making the Waterford defence appear slow and clumsy. This time, instead of crossing it, he takes on their goalie. The poor kid doesn't stand a chance. Rex slides it past him like he's asleep.

2-0 to the Ferndale Foxes. At half-time, things are looking good. We gather round our old coach, Darren.

'You're doing a great job out there, lads!' he says in his usual upbeat manner. He's always positive, even when we lose. That's one thing I'll miss. 'Keep it up! I couldn't be prouder of you!'

I take a long drink of water. I'm pleased, but I'm also tired. I've been sprinting up and down the pitch like crazy and I'm not sure I'll be able to keep it up in the second half. My feet are cold and wet, and that's not helping: the holes in my boots have let in mud and my socks are saturated. They make a squelching noise as I walk, and one of my heels is getting a blister. The sooner I get new boots, the better.

We take our positions and Waterford kick off. For a while, the two teams seem evenly matched. Pass, tackle, pass. The ball keeps switching sides. It's not long, though, before Waterford's quick passes grind us down. Our guys in midfield are getting frustrated.

They're wearing us out!

My teammates are out of breath. Rex has slowed to half his usual pace. He's spent, all of his earlier brilliance now fading. Ashar has sweat pouring down his face as he chases his mark. Dave has stopped smiling. Our team is losing heart and Waterford are taking advantage.

'Come on, guys! Chin up!' shouts Darren, trying to spur us on. But it's energy we need, not encouragement.

Our defence does the best job it can as our opponents descend on us in force.

Miles, our keeper, can see what's happening. He's calm and focused, barking out orders. 'Watch the guy on the left!' he shouts to Harry, who's hesitating as two players come rushing towards him.

It's too late.

Waterford thunder past, taking a shot which sends Miles sprawling in the mud. He makes contact with the ball, but not enough to stop it.

2-1.

We're only fifteen minutes in to the second half. The tide has turned. If we want to stay in the lead, then we have to fight for it.

I glance over at Sammo. He's observing the game, showing no emotion. I wonder what he's thinking.

My teammates are much easier to read. Brandon has a look of grim determination. Rex is holding his head, frustrated. Dave is fiddling with his captain's armband. I reach down and pull my socks even higher, so they almost reach my shorts. We can't let this one slip away.

Waterford come at us again and again. We fight them off, one small victory after another, but we're exhausted, and it shows. Some of our tackles are nothing short of desperate. It's a miracle no-one gets a red card.

They manage to take a few more shots. Thankfully, Miles is sharp and blocks them. But he can't keep it up forever.

How we make it to full-time I'll never know. But we do. We scrape through, holding on to our early lead. 2-1. I collapse on the muddy ground, completely worn out.

It might be a win, but it almost ended differently.

I'm glad it's over.

***

We say our goodbyes to Darren. This time I wish him luck. Everyone is emotional. When we come away, I see Sammo waiting. He looks unimpressed.

'Well?' asks Dave. 'What did you think?'

'You're not great.'

'But will you coach us?' I blurt out, desperate.

'Depends on whether you'll pay me sixty quid a week.'

'SIXTY!' I can't hide my outrage.

'Yep. That's what I charge. And you do whatever I say. No chatting back.'

I'm furious, but also torn. Rex lowers his eyes, embarrassed that his brother is trying to rip us off.

'Ok,' says Dave. 'It's a deal.'

'Great,' replies Sammo. 'Bring the first payment on Tuesday. And make sure you're on time. You boys have a lot of work to do.'

'You realise we won that game, right?' I can't help pointing it out.

'Ha, that wasn't a win, Jeddy! That was a fluke! You barely survived out there.' Sammo smirks at me. 'If that game was ten minutes longer, you'd have been lucky to draw.'

I want to argue, but deep down I know he's right. And that just makes it worse.

Dave and I watch him leave with Rex.

'Sixty quid a week? He's mugging us off!' I kick the ground.

'Maybe he just needs the money?' shrugs Dave. 'It's

not great, but what choice do we have? At least the Foxes live to fight another day!'

'I guess.'

Despite Dave's optimism, I have a terrible feeling about Sammo that just won't go away.

6. RAIN

Getting up at 7am is harsh. I know I shouldn't complain, but I hate it. Worse still, I can hear heavy rain on the window as I turn off my alarm.

I climb out of bed and drag on the base layers and the lime green Liverpool kit before trudging down the stairs.

Stuffing my feet into battered trainers, I steel myself as I open the back door. A blast of cold air hits me in the face. I know how I have to play this. When you're going to get drenched, there's no point trying to avoid it. I pull up the socks as high as they'll go, no longer caring if I look stupid. I need as much protection as I can get.

The moment I step outside, the water hammers onto my shirt, making me shiver. I jump on my bike, keen to get moving. I've not even made it to the road before I realise that something is wrong. The front tyre is dragging: I have a puncture.

Cursing, I throw the bike back into the shed. Then I run to the newsagents, worried that I won't make it on time. I crash into the shop with one minute to spare. He has no idea how stressed I am. He just hands me the bag.

'Your mum not giving you a lift today?' he asks, surprised to see me so wet.

'She doesn't have a car,' I admit. 'But it's ok, it's only rain.'

He probably thinks my bike is outside and I decide not to tell him about the puncture. I don't want him thinking that I'm unreliable or that the papers won't get delivered. I can just about run the route before I get the bus to school.

As soon as I set off, I find that jogging with a bag of heavy papers is difficult. It keeps banging against my legs and backside. I have to hold it with both hands. But what can I do? The shopkeeper won't let me keep the paper round if I can't hack it. I grit my teeth and carry on.

Delivering the first few papers isn't too bad. I'm soaked to the skin but running keeps me warm. It must also be good for my fitness level. That's what I try to tell myself, anyway, but it's a challenge to stay positive.

I'm cold, wet and miserable and by the time I'm down to my last paper, I want to quit.

Can I get away without going to Briar's farm? I doubt it. There's a good chance the farmer will phone up to ask the newsagent about his missing paper. Then I'll get the sack. I have to do it; however grim it is.

The thing is, I'm running out of time. If I don't get a move on, I'll miss the bus. I pick up the pace as I run along the lane.

I'm struggling for breath by the time I reach the turning to Briar's Farm. I can't remember the last time I had to run this distance. I stop for a moment, coughing and retching at the side of the road. Then I carry on.

The farm track is worse than I expect. It's been torn to pieces by tractor tyres and farm machinery. I slip and slide, through ankle-deep puddles and slimy mud. There's no point being a pansy about it. I need to think like Miles, the Foxes' goalie. He loves getting muddy. He'd think this was fun.

But he's not the one having to do it.

Shep barks as I approach the farmhouse, but this time his tail is wagging, and he's being friendly. That's good as there's no sign of the farmer. I drop the paper through the letterbox and head off.

All done! Now I can go home. The bag is a lot lighter. That should make it easier, but I'm shattered.

Picking up my pace, I misjudge my step on the track. I stack it, rolling sideways in the brown slime. It's freezing cold and soaks right through my kit.

I curse and climb to my feet, half of my body now covered in mud. And I mean covered. You can't see skin or neon green or anything else. Just brown muck. I wipe my hands on my shirt, making even more of a mess.

Can today get any worse?

It turns out it can. When I make it back to the village, several kids are already standing at the bus stop. Normally I'm home before now, but this time I have an audience as I run past in my mud-soaked Liverpool kit. They laugh and jeer. I smile at them, but my cheeks are burning.

I get to my house at 8.14am and I strip off the filthy gear as fast as I can. My bus leaves in five minutes.

I don't have time to shower or eat breakfast, even though I feel grim. I wash my face and try to rinse the worst of the mud out of my hair before throwing on my uniform. Then I grab my schoolbag, sling it over my shoulder, and head out.

Getting soaked is bad enough the first time, but getting drenched twice within the hour is horrible. My thin coat isn't waterproof, and the rain goes straight through. I hate this. I hate being wet, and cold, and poor. I fight back the tears as I run.

I turn the corner just in time to see the bus driving off, leaving me in the street. Some of the older students laugh and point out the window.

I want to give up. I want to go home and have a warm shower and take the day off school. But quitting is not in my DNA. That's not what I do. I'm tougher than that; I always have been. I'm wet and dirty. So what? I've missed the bus, but it's not the end of the world.

In a few hours' time, none of it will matter. I just have to get through this.

***

I get on the next bus. The driver shouldn't let me use my pass at this time of day, but I look so pathetic and hopeless that he can't say no.

The journey takes twenty minutes, and the bus is warm and comfortable. I should feel rested, but my legs ache as I trudge through the school gates. The torrential rain has eased to a light drizzle. I can't even be bothered to jog the short distance up the school driveway.

If you arrive after the bell, there's only one way in. That means trouble.

'Late again, Jed?' asks Mrs Powell, the school secretary.

'Sorry. I missed the bus.' I don't explain why. It wouldn't make any difference.

'You know what that means?'

'Detention,' I sigh.

She hands me one of the pink slips. 'Tomorrow, after school.'

'Sure, thanks.' I'm not sure why I'm thanking her.

'And Jed?'

'Yes, miss?'

'Don't be late.'

I give her a weak smile, then tug my tatty organiser out of my bag to check what the first lesson is. Our school has this stupid two-week timetable, so every week is different. My heart sinks when I see that it's PE.

Don't get me wrong: normally, I love it. But there are two reasons I don't want to do sport right now. First, I'm knackered after running the whole paper round. There's no way I'm going to have the energy to play football. And second, in my hurry to catch the bus I realise that I've forgotten my kit. I hope our teacher is in a good mood.

As I push open the door to the changing rooms, the other kids are heading out to the field.

'Jed!' says Mr Davidson. 'How nice of you to join us.'

'Sorry I'm late, sir.' I realise it's best to come straight out with it. 'And I forgot my kit.'

'Not a great start, is it, Jed?' He frowns at me. Usually, I'm one of his star players. 'You better find some in the lost property box and get yourself out on to the field sharpish. You'll do one lap for every minute you take.'

'Yes, sir.'

I dash over to the large box in the corner, its contents

spewing on to the floor. I rummage around, hunting for anything that's my size. It's all pretty grim. Who knows how many times it's been worn already?

I drag out one of the red sports shirts, some grubby white shorts and yellow football socks that are encrusted with mud. Now I just need boots. There are loads of them, but finding the right size isn't easy. As I plunge to the bottom, something catches my eye.

It can't be. But it is. A pair of Nexus Cheetahs. They cost like a hundred quid. And these look brand new. They're a size too big, but so what? I put on a second pair of football socks, then they're perfect. It seems my luck is changing.

I jog out to the pitch.

'That was five minutes, Jed. You owe me five laps. Then you're on Alfie's team.'

'Yes, sir.'

I force myself around the field, my legs like lead. This is going to be tough, but at least he didn't give me another detention. And for once, my feet are dry. The new boots are amazing. I could get used to this.

When I finally join the game, it's a lot of fun. The teams are well-matched and no-one is taking it too seriously. I take some shots against Miles.

'You can do better than that, Jed!' he teases, as he

snatches the ball out of the air.

'Sure,' I grin. 'I'm just warming up.'

And it's true. As the game gets going, I play better and better. Even though I'm tired, the boots are incredible. I can get a grip with them and don't keep sliding over. It's like they're moulded to my feet.

By the time I get back to the changing room, I'm torn. I don't steal stuff. Never. I've had enough stuff taken over the years to know how it feels. But I can't put the boots back in the box. They're too nice.

Besides, it's not technically stealing if they're in lost property, right? Some rich kid probably lost them ages ago and went out and bought a fresh pair. Chances are, they've forgotten all about them.

In the end, I compromise. I won't keep them, but I will borrow them. Just for a few weeks, until I can afford some of my own. Then I'll bring them back. Surely that's fair? But I still feel guilty as I stuff them into my bag and head to the next lesson.

7. CIRCUITS

When I get home from school, I want to collapse in front of the TV, but tonight is our first training session with Sammo. It's the third time today I've put on a football kit; I'm getting worse than Brandon.

I don't care about that. That's not what bothers me. The truth is, I'm spent. Never have I felt so shattered. My legs ache like crazy after all I put them through this morning.

I groan as I realise I can't even bike to the ground: I still have a puncture. It's only a ten-minute walk, but it fills me with dread.

I need energy, and fast.

I open the kitchen cupboards, hunting for something to eat. A pile of bills lies on the side, bright red letters demanding urgent payments. I wonder if I should offer mum some of the money from my paper round, if it would help get the bailiffs off her back. But once I've paid Sammo, I'll barely have any left.

I root out half a pack of biscuits and wolf them down.

It's not the healthiest snack, but I'll take what I can get. Then I grab the borrowed boots and head off, wondering what Sammo will be like as a coach.

***

It's stopped raining, but the field is as muddy as it gets.

There's also a strange atmosphere. Everyone is speaking in hushed tones. I head over to where Dave is standing with Miles.

'What's going on?' I ask.

'We're waiting for Sammo to get here. I think we're all a bit on edge.'

'Yeah, me too. And I'm shattered.'

'How come?' Dave sounds concerned. He's a good mate like that: he cares.

'I got a puncture this morning. Had to do my paper round on foot. Before we had PE.'

'Ouch. Is it sorted now?'

'Nope. Can't fix it,' I admit. 'I don't have a clue how to do it. I was hoping I could borrow your bike until it's mended?'

'Sure, I guess,' says Dave, 'but I'll need it back.' Dave's lent me stuff before. He knows there's a high chance he'll never see it again.

'Just for a few days,' I assure him. 'Until I work something out.'

'Ok. Come and get it after training.'

'Cheers.'

Our conversation comes to an end as Sammo drives into the car park much too fast, screeching to a halt. He gets out and opens up the back.

'You,' he barks at Brandon, 'get over here.' Sammo hands him an enormous bag and a stack of training cones. 'Put it over by the goal.'

Brandon does as he's told, stumbling under the weight of the heavy equipment. Sammo follows him, empty-handed.

'Right, gather round.' We all draw close, a little nervous. 'You got my first payment?'

Dave draws a pile of cash out of his tracksuit pocket and hands it over. Sammo counts it. I haven't given my share; I can't until I'm paid for the paper round.

Dave catches my eye. 'Don't worry,' he says, quietly. 'I've subbed you for now. You can pay me back next week.'

Great. This new deal has only just started and I'm already in debt. Just like my mum.

Sammo pockets the money and glances around, working out how to begin. 'You boys are a shambles,' he says. It's not the most encouraging start. 'Look at the state of you. Half of you aren't even in proper kit. So, from now on, you show up to training on time. You wear your training shirts, shorts, socks, shin-pads, just as you would for a match. You want to play like a pro, you dress like a pro. Got it?'

A few of the boys appear annoyed but no-one objects. We don't wear shin-pads for training. Seems like that's about to change. There's a mumble of assent.

'Second, you do everything I tell you. You call me "coach". No talking back, no stupid questions, no complaints. If you're gonna whine, then I'm wasting my time with you. If I hear anything negative, then you'll be doing laps until you puke. Or you can go home and never come back.'

I swallow hard. No-one speaks.

'Let's be clear about something else,' continues Sammo. 'Your performance on Saturday was appalling, and you know why? You're all unfit. You need to get off your butts and do some exercise. So, for the next few weeks that's what we're doing. I'm going to work you hard, and you're gonna hate me. I don't care. I hope you're ready to break a sweat?'

I'm not, but I can hardly say that. The last thing I want to do is fitness training. No-one else looks keen either.

'The response I'm after is *yes, coach*,' sneers Sammo. 'So, let's try that again. I hope you're ready to break a sweat?'

'Yes, coach,' a few of us mutter.

'We're going to work on that. This time, if I'm not sensing a hundred percent enthusiasm then you'll all be doing press-ups in the goal-mouth.'

I glance over. It's the worst part of the pitch: a deep puddle stretches from one post to the other.

'So, one last time,' carries on Sammo, with a wicked grin. 'Are you ready to break a sweat?'

'YES, COACH,' we all shout, as though we're marines.

'That's better. Let's warm up with ten laps. Off you trot. Make sure you don't come last.'

Ten laps just to warm up? That's extreme, but we race off. No-one wants to risk being left behind. I've only done half of it before I feel like I'm about to throw up. I stagger on, trying to keep pace with Miles, who's taking it slow and steady.

'Whose idea was it to ask Sammo to coach us?' he asks, as we run. 'Remind me to give them a good kicking later.'

'That would be Dave,' I reply, not wanting to own up to my part in the decision.

'Figures.'

We don't have the energy to say much else.

I'm not gonna lie: I can't keep up. One lap later, I fall behind, slowing to a walk. Sammo's not impressed.

'Need a rest, Jeddy boy?' he asks me, raising his eyebrows as I draw near.

'Yeah, sorry,' I gasp, coughing.

'Yeah, sorry, *coach*,' he points out. He's enjoying this.

'Yeah, sorry, coach,' I repeat.

'Ok, why don't you have a lie down?' he suggests. There's something about the way he says it which troubles me.

'I'll be fine, coach. Just need a few minutes to catch my breath.' I'm standing by the goal, leaning forward with my hands on my knees.

'It wasn't a suggestion,' says Sammo. 'If you've stopped running, then you lie down. That's the rule.'

I glance at the muddy ground. 'In that?'

'No questions, remember? You do what I say.'

I look at him, checking he's serious. It appears he is. 'Yes, coach.'

I drop to the floor, planting my backside in the wet mud. As I lean back, it soaks through the back of my shirt. I shiver on the ground.

'There you go. Enjoy your rest,' sneers Sammo. 'You can stay there until the others have finished.'

Fortunately, that only takes a couple of minutes.

'Right, get up.' Sammo kicks a puddle, sending filthy water flying in my direction. 'Any complaints?'

'No, coach.' I clamber to my feet, my shirt sticking to my back. It's like being in the army. The other lads are puffing and panting.

'You get three minutes to rest,' barks Sammo. 'Breathe deeply. Then we're starting some circuits.' He heads onto the pitch to lay out cones.

'Well, this is fun,' says Brandon, drily.

'I tried to warn you,' says Rex. I get the feeling he's going to say that a lot.

'It'll be fine,' says Dave, but even he doesn't sound convinced.

'I think I'm gonna puke,' complains Theo.

There's a pause as we try to catch our breath.

'New boots, Jed?' asks Brandon. 'Nexus Cheetahs! Very nice!'

'They looked better before I ran through that,' I say, nodding towards the pitch.

'That paper round must pay a lot,' jokes Theo. 'How on earth did you afford those?' He wouldn't have asked any of the other boys, and it annoys me.

'None of your business.'

'Tristan had a pair like that,' says Ashar. 'They got nicked at school.'

'You saying I stole them?' I lock eyes with him. 'Just because I'm poor doesn't mean I'm a thief!'

I don't know why I make such an issue of it; that's exactly what I've done, in a way. Maybe that's why I'm so defensive.

'No.' Ashar backs down. 'I was just saying he had the same boots, that's all.' But he looks at me, suspicious. He's not convinced.

Our three minutes are up. Sammo blows a whistle and before we know it, he's got us doing more exercise.

'I'm going to die,' complains Brandon. I'm kneeling on the ground, holding his ankles as he does twenty sit-ups.

'Me too,' agrees Rex, who's in the same position.

'Well, you have to admit he has a point,' offers Dave. 'We are all unfit.'

'Yeah, but that's not why he's doing this,' pants Rex. 'He just wants to cause us pain.'

He might be right, but it doesn't matter. Sammo is our coach and we have to deal with it. By the time the session ends, I can barely stand. I'm not the only one.

We're in a line as Sammo paces in front of us like a drill sergeant. 'Another lacklustre performance from you all today,' he says. 'I expect better on Thursday. If you can't hack it, don't show up.'

A few of the guys look tempted. Dave and I might

need to persuade them to stick it out, for a bit longer at least. We're heading off when Sammo calls me over.

'Yes, coach?' I ask, wondering why I've been singled out.

'Jed, you have real promise,' he says. 'Natural talent. I could see that on Saturday. I'm going to give you some personal training.'

I'm not sure what to say. I'm surprised by the compliment and normally I'd love more football training, but this session has been absolute hell.

'I don't know...' I begin, but Sammo cuts me off.

'No complaining. No excuses. Remember?'

'Sure, I guess.'

'Meet me here at 7.00pm tomorrow,' he says.

'But it'll be dark,' I object. 'I won't be able to see anything.'

'It'll be fine. Trust me. And don't tell the others. We don't want them getting jealous. Ok?'

I sigh and say the only thing I can: 'Yes, coach.'

8. TROUBLE

Dave's bike is a dream. It gives me hope. As I ride back from his house, I don't feel so bad. I dump it in the shed and go through the back door. Mum's in the kitchen, making a cup of tea.

'Jed! You're filthy!' she cries. 'You're not coming in here like that!'

I glance down. She has a point. I step outside and start stripping off.

'If you think I'm washing all that for you, you've got another thing coming,' she calls out. 'I don't have time to clean two football kits a day. If you want to keep rolling in the mud, then you can sort it.'

'Sure, no problem.' I try not to sound annoyed. I know she's up to her eyeballs with work, but I can't help thinking that I'm the only boy on the team who has to wash his own clothes.

Now I'm down to my boxers, I go back in. I bundle the dirty kit into the washing machine, along with the Liverpool strip from earlier.

'How was training?' mum asks kindly, probably feeling guilty that the first thing she did was yell at me.

'It was torture,' I reply. 'Sammo's coaching us now Darren's gone. He made us do circuits.'

'Hard luck.' She thinks I'm exaggerating. She has no idea. 'Want a cup of tea?'

'Nah, I'm just gonna shower.'

'Don't use all the hot water.'

Yeah, that's another thing. We have to watch how much of it we use. It all costs money.

I stand under the warm shower, letting it wash away my pain and frustration, along with the muck. It's been a hard day, but I figure things can only get better from here.

Tomorrow I'm going to have to wear the fluorescent-yellow-and-black-striped kit for my paper round, as the Liverpool one won't be dry. But I have Dave's bike so I should finish early and no-one will see me.

Also, I've survived training, and Sammo thinks I show promise. While I'm not sure about having extra sessions with him, I guess it's a good sign that he's volunteering his time. Maybe he's not just in it for the money.

Things are definitely on the up.

Most importantly, we've saved the Foxes. Against all the odds, we've done it. And that's all that matters.

***

With Dave's bike, I finish the paper round in record time. I even get a proper breakfast before I catch the bus. When I arrive in my form room for registration, I feel upbeat.

But my life is never easy. I should have known something bad would happen.

'Ah Jed, Mr Davidson wants to see you,' says my tutor.

'What, right now?' I ask, a little surprised.

'Yes, immediately. He should be in his office.'

I jog across to the sports centre, wondering what it's about. Hopefully, he just needs to tell me about a new football competition or ask me to play in a match.

No such luck.

Mr Davidson is sitting at his desk in the cramped office.

'You want to see me, sir?'

'Ah, Jed. Yes. Take a seat.' He indicates the chair opposite. I move some training bibs to the side, then slump into it.

'I'm afraid someone has made a serious accusation,' says the teacher. 'Apparently you have a new pair of football boots?'

'Sort of.' My face is burning hot. 'That's not illegal, is it?'

'That depends. These wouldn't be Nexus Cheetahs, would they?' He's calm, but he intends to sort this out. There doesn't seem to be much point denying it.

'Yes, sir.'

'Do you mind telling me where you got them?'

I can't lie to him. 'Lost property,' I mumble. 'I found them when you told me to get some kit.'

'Ah, I see.' He relaxes a little. 'So, you find a nice pair of boots in the box, and decide that it won't hurt if you keep them?'

I stare at the floor and give a small nod. 'Sorry, sir. They just fitted so well and I didn't think anyone would care.'

'Sadly, they did. Tristan spent a hundred quid on those. He reckons that someone took them out of his bag.'

'I didn't. I swear!'

'I believe you. But that doesn't mean what you did was ok.'

'No, sir.'

'Do you have them with you?'

I reach into my backpack and pull them out. They don't look so good now they're covered in mud.

Mr Davidson lets out a low whistle. 'Well, you've got some use out of those! You can't give them back to Tristan like that. At break-time you need to clean them, thoroughly. And then you're going to return them to him in person, along with a heartfelt apology.'

'Yes, sir.' I can't stand Tristan, but I can hardly object.

'I expect him to have them back by afternoon registration. I will check.'

I nod.

'Jed, it's not like you to do something like this. Is everything ok at home?'

'Sure. It's fine, sir. I just need some new boots.'

He looks at me sadly. He'd probably buy me some if he was allowed. He's that kind of teacher. But there are rules against that sort of thing.

'Ok, Jed. Well, you clean the boots and we'll call the matter closed. Don't do it again.'

'I won't, sir. I promise.'

I know that he's disappointed. As I walk out of his office, I feel as dirty as the boots.

***

Cleaning them is torture.

I'm standing over the sink in the toilets, scrubbing at them with my fingers, not sure what else I can use to dislodge the muck.

The worst part is I'm never going to get to wear them again. This must be what servants used to feel like in the olden days: having to clean things they couldn't afford, doing everyone else's dirty work.

When I finish, they're a lot better. Not like new, but decent. I head into the playground and hunt around for Tristan. He's standing with a group of mates over by the wall. I make my way over.

'Look who it is, the little thief!' spits Tristan, before I've had a chance to speak. 'Come to nick something else?'

Seems that word has got out about the boots. I pull them out of my bag. 'I didn't steal them from you. Honest.'

'Yeah, sure,' he says sarcastically. He snatches them from me, then holds them away in disgust. 'They're dripping wet!'

'That's because I just cleaned them.'

'I'm not sure if I want them after your skanky feet have been in them,' he taunts.

'I said I'm sorry, alright. You've got them back now. It was just a misunderstanding.'

'A misunderstanding? You took a brand-new pair of boots out my bag!'

'Actually, I found them in lost property,' I explain. 'I didn't know they were yours.'

'So, why'd you keep them?'

'That's where he gets all of his stuff,' jokes Bryant, and the others laugh.

'How about we take something of yours?' suggests Tristan. 'So you know what it feels like?'

Before I can answer, Bryant grabs my bag. He empties it onto the floor. He spreads the stuff out with his foot, trying to find something to take. 'You don't own *anything* decent, do you?'

I turn red and stay silent. Even to my eyes, it just looks like a pile of rubbish.

'You're pathetic,' concludes Tristan. 'You're a loser, and a thief. You watch yourself.'

He walks off, trampling my books as he goes. Once him and his mates have left, I gather it up.

It's not easy being poor, but I rarely get this level of abuse. I guess this time it's my own fault.

I trudge off, thoroughly depressed.

9. WINDOW

I wait by the goalposts. It's gone 7pm, and it's properly dark. The field is deserted.

I'm ready for my extra training with Sammo, even though I can't work out how I'm going to see the ball. I had to wear my orange kit because everything else is still drying, but I'm properly kitted out so he can't complain: shorts, socks, shin-pads, the works.

He skids into the car park, five minutes late, his headlights blinding me. As my eyes adjust, I see him beckoning me over.

'You're looking sharp,' he comments.

'Sure. Just like you asked.' I'm keen to get on his good side. 'I think it's a good thing, making us more professional and stuff.'

'Good. Get in.' He gestures to the passenger seat.

'Why?'

'No questions, remember? Just do as I say.'

'Yes, coach.'

He drives off while I'm struggling with the seat belt.

The music blasts out of the stereo. He turns it off as we drive down the road, out of the village.

'Where are we going?' I ask. I can't help asking questions; I'm nervous.

'I need your help with something. That's ok, isn't it?'

'Sure, I guess.'

'Don't worry, it's right up your street,' he says.

That doesn't reassure me.

We drive to a nearby village and stop next to a large house hidden amongst the trees.

'Out,' says Sammo.

I climb out of the car. He leads me up the long driveway. The place feels deserted. I shiver in the shadows.

'Who lives here?' I ask.

'It's a mate's house,' he shrugs. 'Problem is, his parents are away on holiday and he's locked himself out. That's why we need your help.'

I'm uneasy. 'Why me? What can I do?'

'You, Jeddy boy, are the skinniest runt I know. There's a tiny window that's been left open. I need you to climb through it and open the front door for us.'

'You want me to break in?'

'No, because it's not breaking in when you have the owner's permission, is it?' says Sammo, like I'm stupid.

'So, where is your mate?' I ask. We head through a side-gate into the back garden. Sammo uses his phone to light the way.

'He's at work. Enough questions. All you have to do is get through that and find a key to open the door.' He points to the window. It's tiny, and way above my head, but at least it's on the ground floor.

'I'm not sure I should.'

'You don't need to be sure. You just need to do as you're told. That's the deal, remember?'

It shouldn't matter. But I think of the Foxes, and what it would be like if the team folded. I can't face it. I push my doubts aside.

'Yeah, I remember,' I mumble. 'Sorry, coach.'

'That's better.' He ruffles my hair, like I'm a dog. 'Now, take off your boots and I'll give you a boost.'

I do as he says. He cups his hands so I can step into them, then lifts me up. I stick my head in the window. It's such a tiny gap I'm not sure that I'll fit. I ease my way forwards, finding myself in a downstairs toilet. As I drag my legs behind me and try to get the right way up, one of my feet somehow ends up in the toilet bowl. I curse and pull it out, my sock dripping.

That's just great.

I switch on the light and make my way down the polished hallway to the front door, leaving a trail of wet footprints.

I thought the hard part was over, but I can't open the door from the inside. There's no sign of a key, so I return to the window where Sammo is waiting.

'It's locked and there's no key!' I shout.

'Try the back,' he orders, 'and check the kitchen drawers.'

I swallow hard and pad through to a gleaming kitchen-diner which is bigger than my house. It takes a few minutes of hunting around in the utility room, but Sammo knows what he's talking about. Behind the cutlery tray is a set of keys. One of them fits the back door.

I've barely turned the handle before Sammo pushes his way inside. He's put on a pair of black gloves.

'This isn't your mate's house, is it?' I ask, weakly.

'I knew you'd work it out,' he says with a grin. 'You might as well help me find the valuables. Here.' He thrusts a strong canvas bag at me. 'Fill that with anything expensive. Small stuff only. Things I'll be able to sell.'

'I'm not a thief!'

'Really? How come you got those boots then? I heard you stole them off another lad.'

I shrug. I don't owe him an explanation.

He shakes his head. 'Ok, just wait here. Don't go

anywhere.' He dashes up the stairs, taking them two at a time. I'm shaking, too afraid to move.

He's only gone a few minutes, but it feels like a lifetime. The bag he's holding bulges and clinks. He pushes it at me. 'Take this to the car. Wait for me there.'

I gulp and slip out, glad to have an excuse to leave. Sammo left the car unlocked, so I open the back and throw in the bag. I glance around, but there's no sign of life in the houses nearby. I climb into the passenger seat to wait out the rest of the nightmare.

A few more minutes pass. I feel like I'm gonna throw up.

What is he doing?

Sammo strolls out, all casual, a bag over his shoulder. It's almost comical, like something from a cartoon. All he needs is a black-and-white striped t-shirt and an eye-mask and he'd really look the part.

He jumps into the driver's seat and starts up the engine. 'Good work, mate. That's a nice little haul!' He says it like I'm his accomplice.

I stay silent.

'What's up?' he asks. 'Not being a wuss, are we?'

'No,' I mumble. 'But you lied to me. I want nothing to do with this.'

'Well, that's hard luck. From now on, you're my little

helper.'

I taste bile in my throat. 'I'm never doing that again.'

Sammo laughs. 'It's not like you have a choice.'

'What do you mean?'

'I mean, Jeddy boy, that if you don't carry on helping me with my little business venture, then two things are going to happen. First, no more football for you. And second, the police will get a tip-off about the burglary that leads them to your front door.'

I glance at him in horror. 'You wouldn't?'

'Believe me, I would. You know how easy it would be? Your fingerprints are all over that place.'

He's right. They are. It would be easy to frame me.

'I'll tell them you made me do it.' I squirm in my seat.

'You could try, but who are they going to believe? The guy reporting the crime he saw, as he drove through the village, or a council-estate brat like you?'

I stare out the window.

'From now on,' carries on Sammo, 'we're in this together. I think extra training might become a regular thing. It's a good alibi. If anyone asks where I was tonight, you know what to tell them.'

I still don't speak. There's nothing to say.

'Don't forget I'm still your coach, Jed,' he points out. 'You do as I say. Don't tell anyone about this. That way, you keep playing football and stay out of juvey. That's what you want, isn't it?'

That is what I want. Playing football and staying out of prison are both high on my list of priorities.

'Yeah,' I mutter.

'Yes, *coach*,' he demands.

'Yes, *coach*,' I reply, through gritted teeth.

He grins at me. 'That's much better. Good boy.'

I swallow hard. This is not good.

10. SPECTATORS

On Saturday we have our next game, but I can't get my head straight. I should be excited. We're playing against Welbeck, our local rivals. We need to win. But I hate being around Sammo.

Our practice on Thursday was another grim circuit training session where he yelled at us non-stop.

I can't stand him, but I can't get away.

I'm feeling glum as I sit in the car. Dave's dad is taking us, like always.

'You ok, Jed?' he asks. 'You're quiet.'

'I guess. I've got a lot on my mind.'

'Anything you want to talk about?'

'I dunno,' I admit. I can hardly tell him I've been thieving. He knows I'm rough around the edges, but he's always been decent to me.

'Dave said you've been having trouble with your bike? Is that what's worrying you?'

'Yeah.' It isn't my main stress, but at least I can speak about that. 'I got a puncture on my paper round and don't know how to fix it.'

'Ah,' he says, glancing at me in the rear-view mirror. 'Well, why not bring it round to our place after the match and I'll take a look?'

'That would be amazing. Thanks!'

My bike might not be the biggest of my problems, but I'm a lot happier as we pull into the Welbeck ground. Dave and I jump out and jog over to the rest of our team.

'Dave! Jed! Alright?'

'Fine,' says Dave. 'I can't wait to crush Welbeck. Let's see if all this fitness training pays off.'

'I could barely walk after our last practice,' complains Miles. 'Sammo worked us so hard, it hurt whenever I went up the stairs.'

'Me too,' chips in Brandon. 'He can't keep doing that. He's gonna kill us!'

'You're lucky,' mutters Rex. 'You don't have to live with him.'

I shudder at the thought. However bad my situation is, I wouldn't want to swap.

'Hey lads, watch your stuff!' I turn to see Tristan strolling past with some of the other Welbeck players. 'Jed might take something while you're not looking!'

His mates laugh and one of them spits at the ground in my direction. I feel like I'm gonna explode.

Dave pulls on my shirt. 'Ignore them. Save it until we're on the pitch. I think three goals will be enough to wipe that smile off his face, don't you?'

He's right. I let out a deep breath.

Sammo saunters over and gathers us. 'Well lads,' he says, 'it's showtime. I don't want to see anyone holding back. Nail these losers. And just so you know: if any of you even appears tired, we'll be doing more circuit training. Even harder than before.'

There are some muffled groans.

'I'll do you a deal,' continues Sammo. 'If you win this match, and you're not too knackered by the end, then we'll play some football at practice. If you lose, or slow down, then I'm gonna run you boys into the ground. Ok?'

Threats. That's just what we need.

'Yes, coach.' The response isn't enthusiastic. We break away and jog onto the pitch, determined to win for all the wrong reasons.

Welbeck are a tough side. They're not clean or professional, they're just sly and brutal. They play hard. Last time we played them, Dave came away with an injury that put him out of action for two weeks. The ref didn't even give us a free kick.

As we take our places, they eyeball us, like they're

working out which one of us they're going to take down first. Tristan is opposite me, a mean expression on his face. I might as well have a bulls-eye on my back.

A few seconds later, we're off. Welbeck are rushing into our half, but the defenders do their job. The ball comes sailing towards Rex, who starts sprinting up the wing. He makes mincemeat out of the midfielder who tries to slide him, jumping over the outstretched leg with ease. But now, two thuggish defenders are blocking his path.

'Back!' shouts Dave. Rex isn't selfish. Either that, or he doesn't fancy his chances. He sends the ball in Dave's direction. It doesn't stay there for long. It's passed forward to Brandon, who crosses to me. I hurtle towards the goal. The keeper is off his line, coming out to meet me.

I know exactly what to do.

I pull back my foot, preparing to chip it over the keeper's head. But before I do, Tristan crashes in to my side. I land roughly on the ground and appeal to the ref for support, but he doesn't blow the whistle. Tristan takes the ball and boots it up the field.

'Unlucky, loser!' he says. As I try to get up, he sweeps my hand from under me, leaving me sprawling in the mud. No-one is looking our way. They're all focused on the action at the other end.

'Leave me alone,' I say, sounding pathetic.

'I can see why you were so desperate to steal my boots,' he smirks. 'How old are those?'

I glance down at my feet, embarrassed. My orange socks are visible through the large holes.

'You're such a tramp.' Satisfied that he's crushed my self-esteem, he jogs away.

I want to hit him, but I know I can't. A red card doesn't get you anywhere. Dave catches my eye. He can see I'm upset. He's checking that I'm not about to lose it.

'I'm fine,' I mouth at him across the pitch.

He nods and turns his attention back to the action. I remember what he said earlier. The best way to teach Tristan a lesson is to win. By a lot.

I focus and get in the zone. The Foxes are getting the right idea. If Welbeck can't tackle us, then they don't have much opportunity to foul us either. We make lots of quick passes.

Before long, I have another chance to score. Rex spins and sends the ball curving towards me. It's the perfect cross, and I'm not going to waste it. Tristan is miles away, and I get the shot in before he can send me flying. It thunders past the goalie, to the back of the net.

1—0 at last!

It's all we manage before the half-time whistle, but it's

enough to give us hope. We're on top of the world as we swig our water and joke around.

We're too confident, and we should know better.

In the second half, things get sketchy. Whatever their coach has said to them during the break, Welbeck are getting rougher by the minute. They lay into us, shoulder-barging and sliding.

We carry on passing as quick as we can. That helps. We're a lot sharper than we were last week. Maybe the fitness training is making a difference.

It's some time before I get the ball, but when I do, I'm on it. We need another goal. A defender runs towards me, and I fake a pass. It distracts him so I can circle past and take a cheeky shot. Their goalie hasn't seen it coming. It slides into the bottom corner.

2—0.

I grin at Tristan as I run past.

'I don't know why you're so pleased with yourself,' he says, slyly. 'Look who just turned up.'

I glance over my shoulder, confused. In the car park, there's a police car. Two officers are getting out.

My legs turn to jelly.

Why are they here? Has Sammo set me up?

I try to keep my mind on the game, but the officers are standing with the other spectators, chatting to some parents. How am I meant to focus now?

Sammo sees that my game has gone to pieces and beckons me over. He puts his hand on the back of my neck as he leans down to whisper in my ear. 'Listen to me, Jeddy boy,' he hisses. 'You need to keep silent. Say nothing, you hear me? I don't know why the cops are here, but keep your cool. Remember our deal.'

I gulp and nod, but my legs won't stop shaking.

'Go to the toilets and calm down,' says Sammo. 'It's going to be fine. Trust me.'

If there's one thing I'll never do, it's trust him. But I do as he says, all the same. I want to throw up. I can't live with the guilt of what I've done, or the constant threat of being found out. But what choice do I have?

I splash water on my face and try to slow my breathing. I head back out, in time to hear the whistle; I missed the end of the match.

'Did we win?' I ask Dave, no longer caring.

'Yes, two nil! Where did you go?'

'I needed the toilet.'

He raises his eyebrows, but doesn't push it.

Our team are huddled near our goal, celebrating. I'm glad we've won, but I can see the police officers approaching. As they get closer, the boys quieten down, wondering what they want.

'Great game, lads,' calls the older one. He's got a friendly face, but it doesn't put me at ease. 'Congratulations on your win! I wonder if we might have a word?'

11. ORANGE

'How can we help?' Sammo appears relaxed as he turns around, like he hasn't a care in the world.

I wish I could stay cool like that. I'm leaning against the goalpost for support, gripping it tightly with one hand. I hope I don't throw up; I look guilty enough as it is.

'I'm Sergeant Brillin. And you lads must be the Ferndale Foxes,' says the officer. 'Is that right?'

'Yeah, that's us,' replies Dave. 'Why'd you ask?'

'Well, I've been trying to track you down.' The officer looms over us. There's something about a police uniform that makes people seem taller than they actually are. 'As far as I can make out, you're the only team around here that play in orange. Is that correct?'

'I guess,' admits Dave. None of us can see why it matters.

'There was a burglary the other night. In a village near here. One neighbour saw a boy your age dressed in a bright orange football kit coming out of the property. You don't know anything about that, do you?'

Sergeant Brillin glances around, weighing us up. I stare at the ground as if I'm not interested. I hope he can't hear my heart thudding in my chest. The others mutter to one another and shake their heads.

'Did it happen on a Saturday?' asks Sammo.

'No. Wednesday night,' says the sergeant.

'Well, officer,' says Sammo, 'I'm afraid you have the wrong lads. These boys only wear orange for matches at the weekend.'

'Fair enough. Well, sorry to bother you. If any of you know more than you're saying, or anything that might be of interest then call us, ok? I'll leave our number with your coach.' Sergeant Brillin hands Sammo a business card. He might as well throw it in the bin.

They're just turning to leave when Tristan shouts: 'Hey, officers, it's Jed that you want! He's always stealing stuff!'

Everyone looks at me. My face is burning now. I feel as though the word 'THIEF' is tattooed on my forehead.

'Know what he's talking about, son?' asks the sergeant.

'He just doesn't like me much,' I say. The words stick in my throat. 'We don't get on.'

I'm not sure he believes me, but he doesn't ask any more questions. He nods and they stroll off, stopping to chat to Tristan on the way.

'Come on,' I urge Dave. 'Let's get out of here.'

We jog over to his dad. I can't get in the car fast enough, and I don't breathe easy until we drive off.

'What was that about?' asks Mr Hughes, as we pass the police car.

'Nothing,' says Dave. 'Some kid broke in to a house last week, wearing an orange kit. Like that's what you'd wear if you were gonna steal something!'

He laughs, and I feel more stupid than ever.

***

Dave's dad drops me home, but tells me to get my bike and take it straight round so he can help me fix the puncture. It doesn't take long to wheel it there.

'That's some puncture, Jed,' he says, kneeling down to inspect the tyre. 'We're going to need a new inner tube.'

'Is that expensive?' I ask.

'About fifty quid.' He sees the shocked look on my face, and he laughs. 'I'm joking! They only cost a couple of quid. I always have a few spares. Don't worry, you can have one.'

I smile, relieved. He has a wicked sense of humour. I stand over him while he shows me how to take the wheel off and remove the tyre.

'You have to let all the air out first,' he explains, 'but you've already done that.' He pulls a small cardboard box off the shelf and removes a black rubber tube from inside. 'This should be the right size for your wheel.'

A couple of minutes later, he's placed it round the rim and fed the valve through the hole. He hands me the pump. 'You can do this bit. It needs inflating.'

I kneel on the garage floor and get to work.

'Dave says that Sammo is working you boys pretty hard,' he comments.

'I guess, but to be fair we are all pretty unfit.'

'I'd coach you myself, if it wasn't for work.'

'You'd be great. I wish you *were* our coach.'

'Dave doesn't,' he says, smiling. 'He'd die of embarrassment.'

I carry on pumping the tyre.

'I'm not sure what I think of Sammo,' carries on Mr Hughes, after a brief pause. 'He's certainly good at football, but he has a bit of a nasty attitude. If you boys have any trouble with him, you will let me know, right?'

'Right. Sure.'

But if we do that, we'll end up with no coach.

'I mean it. The Foxes are a good team, Jed. Don't let him turn you into people you don't want to be.'

I wonder how much he knows. Does he suspect something, or is he just talking about fair play and teamwork and stuff?

Dave's dad detaches the pump and turns the bike the right way up. 'There you go,' he says, patting the saddle. 'Good as new.'

'Thanks,' I say, grateful to have it sorted.

'Is your mum expecting you back?'

'Nah, she's working til nine.'

'Well, do you want to stay for some dinner? I think we're having sausage and mash.'

'Seriously? That would be amazing.'

***

Dinner at Dave's house is the closest thing I know to heaven. It's like a second home to me. His parents seem to like me for some reason. I lap up the family banter and the relaxed atmosphere. I love my mum, but sometimes I wish I lived here instead.

'Roxy says that the police showed up to the football game,' says Katie, Dave's sister, while chopping her sausages into tiny pieces.

'Is that true?' asks their mum, concerned.

'Yeah, apparently some kid has been breaking into

houses,' says Dave. 'Nothing to do with us, but they wanted to ask us about it because he was wearing an orange football kit.'

'How strange.'

'I was thinking,' I say, after a while. 'What do you reckon will happen to that kid the cops are after, if they catch him? Will he go to prison? One for young people, I mean?'

'I doubt it,' says Mr Hughes, rubbing his chin. 'Nowadays he's more likely to get a slap on the wrist or a caution. It all depends on his circumstances and whether he's done anything like that before.'

'So, it's possible? He might?'

'It could happen, I suppose.' Dave's dad looks at me. 'You don't know who it is, do you, Jed?'

'Nah,' I shrug. 'I'm just interested, is all. Sounds like he's our age. Wondered how much trouble he'd be in.'

'Well, if you ask me, that's the wrong question.'

'Yeah?'

'When you become a man, you don't worry so much about the trouble you're going to get in for stuff.'

'How's that?'

'You have to decide what's right. Then do it. And if that gets you into trouble, so be it. It's still the right thing to do.'

'I guess.' I'm not so sure.

'When you become a *man*?' demands Katie. 'How sexist are you, Dad? Do you think women don't care about what's right and wrong?'

'I just meant as you grow older,' backpedals Mr Hughes, flustered. 'It was a bad choice of words.'

'That's like what you said the other day... I can't believe the things that come out of your mouth sometimes...'

Katie and her dad continue to argue for some time.

I'm just relieved that the conversation about the burglary is over. I don't want to talk about it any more. I don't even want to think about it.

And I know one thing for sure: I never want to do anything like that again.

12. THIEF

Sammo has other ideas: he makes that clear at football practice on Tuesday. We're collecting up the cones while the other lads take a drink.

'Don't forget our training session tomorrow.'

My stomach tightens. I look at him, desperate. 'Could we give it a miss?'

'No can do.' He gives me an evil smile. 'Full kit, just like last time. Don't want anyone getting suspicious.'

'That's what almost got me caught!'

'It didn't, though, did it? Besides, you might get a cool nickname. You could be the orange bandit!' He thinks this is all a big joke. My life and my future are something to laugh about.

'Do I have to?' I whine.

'Yeah, or I'll quit and you'll go to jail.'

'You're bluffing.'

'Want to bet on that?' He locks eyes with me.

He's not messing.

***

So, I'm back. Wednesday evening at 7.00pm. And yes, I'm wearing my Foxes kit. All of it, shin-pads included. The only difference is I opted for trainers instead of boots. And yes, I feel like the world's stupidest kid.

Even worse, he's making me wait. At 7.15pm, there's still no sign. I wonder how long I should hang around on the football field in the dark. Just when I'm about to give up and head home, he pulls into the car park and calls me over.

'Ready?'

'I guess. Has another of your stupid mates locked themselves out?'

'I'm not having that kind of cheek,' he shoots back. 'If you're gonna give me attitude, you can start by giving me thirty push-ups.'

You can't be serious!

I'm about to object but think better of it. I drop to the tarmac and do as he says. He glares at me as I stand up. 'Anything else you want to say?'

'No.'

'No, *coach*.'

'No, coach.' If he asked me to beg for a biscuit, I wonder if I'd do it.

'Good, get in.'

I climb in and we drive off, sinking lower as we get further from the village. I don't want to be here, but there's nothing I can do.

The car is in a state, even though it's only a couple of weeks since we cleaned it. Sammo's muddy football boots are in the footwell in front of me, surrounded by fast food wrappers and car park tickets. But there's something else there: a business card. It's the one the police officer gave him on Saturday.

'What's the plan, coach?' I ask, leaning forward to tuck the laces into my trainers.

'You'll enjoy our little session today,' he grins. 'It's something to do with football!'

Maybe we're on our way to do some training? It's not likely, but a boy can hope.

We pull up outside a posh-looking house in Welbeck.

'Want to guess whose house this is?' he asks.

'I have no idea,' I admit. 'Whose?'

'Your mate Tristan's.'

I'm about to point out that he's not my mate, but then I see that Sammo already knows that. 'Why are we here?'

'Well,' says Sammo, leaning back, 'it turns out that Welbeck have their training sessions on Wednesday nights, up at the floodlit all-weather pitch in the middle of town.

And Tristan's mum takes him. So, guess whose house is empty right now?'

'What about his dad?'

'He's at a council meeting. Which makes this place an easy target.'

'I can't do it.'

'Why not? I heard what Tristan said to you at the match. He already accused you of being a thief. He tried to get you in trouble with the cops. Now's the perfect time for a little revenge, don't you think?'

I hate to admit it, but he has a point. Part of me would love to teach Tristan a lesson.

'Besides,' adds Sammo. 'If you don't, then it's not too late to report you for last week's burglary.'

'Ok, I'll do it. Just stop with the threats.'

'Here's what you're going to do,' says Sammo, as if he's talking me through a football drill. 'Just to make sure that the place is empty, you're going to stroll up to the front door and ring the bell.'

'You're not serious?'

'I am. We need to check no-one's home, that they don't have a cleaner or anything.'

'What if someone answers?'

'Say you were playing football in the park round the back, and the ball came over the fence. You want to check their garden for it.'

'Why would I be playing in the dark?'

Sammo shrugs. 'Just for fun. You don't have to explain that. You're a kid. Besides, no-one's gonna question it with you dressed like that.'

'But what if Tristan's in? He knows I don't play around here.'

'He's at practice, remember?'

I let out a long sigh. 'And if nobody answers? What do I do then?'

'Make your way into the back garden. Climb over the gate if necessary. Then unbolt it and let me through. We'll take things from there.'

I sit, staring at the house, unable to move.

'Well, what you waiting for?' Sammo gives me a gentle push. 'Get a move on. We haven't got all day!'

I climb out and jog over. I press the bell and wait, not sure whether I want someone to answer. If they do, I'll have to use my crummy excuse. If they don't, then Sammo's going to make us break into this place. There are no good outcomes.

As it happens, no-one is home. I glance over and give a small shake of my head. He glares at me: *hurry!* I jog around the side and discover the gate isn't locked. When Sammo sees me go through, he strolls over to join me.

A security light switches on, illuminating the garden. It's massive. The lawn has a football goal at one end and there's a decked area with patio furniture and a hot tub in one corner.

'Pretty well off, ain't he?' whispers Sammo, an evil glint in his eye. 'Time we taught the little rich boy and his family a lesson.'

It's weird that Sammo says that, because he's just as rich, but I don't point that out.

'What now?' I ask. My legs are shaking again.

Sammo tries the back door, but it's locked. 'Looks like we need to use a window.'

'But they're all closed.'

Sammo reaches into his trackies and pulls out a long metal bar. 'Time for lesson two, Jeddy boy. This here is a crowbar. It's good at opening things.' He wanders over to the kitchen window.

'Why don't you use it on the door?' I ask, confused.

'Because doors have multiple locks on them,' he says. 'It's much easier to break open a window. They're only held in place by a single catch.'

He levers the bar and without too much effort, the window pops open. He steps back. 'I think I'll let you take it from here.'

'You want me to let you in, like last time?' I ask.

'Nah. This time you take the bag, you get the swag.' He giggles like he's cracked a funny joke. 'Find anything valuable: especially cash and jewellery. Feel free to smash up Tristan's room while you're in there. Just don't take too long.'

He boosts me up to the open window and I scramble through. It's much easier this time as the opening is wider, and I can stand on the kitchen worktop once I'm inside. I drop to the floor and use the light on my phone to look around.

Sammo throws a canvas bag after me. 'Get to work.'

I dash upstairs, heading straight for the main bedroom. A jewellery box has pride of place on the dressing table. I throw it in the bag, then hunt through the drawers. I find some cash, but don't know what else to take, so I wander across the landing to Tristan's room. Even in the low light, I can see that it's a complete tip. He might be rich, but he's no tidier than me. There's a top-of-the-range laptop on his desk, so I swipe that; it's got to be worth something.

Glancing around, I wonder whether to smash stuff up. The idea of getting revenge is tempting. I remember the bullying at school and the way he taunted me during the football match.

I pick up a baseball bat that's leaning against the wall

and run my hand along its smooth edge. There's a shelf full of trophies, and a large mirror on the wall next to it.

I take a deep breath.

I know what I'm going to do.

Even though it's gonna get me in a whole load of trouble.

***

'What took so long?' Sammo is angry when I return. I push the bag through the window before passing out the laptop.

'It took a while to find stuff. I didn't know where to look.'

'You're gonna have to get quicker than that.' He's inspecting the laptop with interest. 'This is decent though, really decent.'

'Help me out, will you?' I ask. My front half is sticking out of the window, but it's a long drop to the ground.

Sammo grabs hold of my torso and drags me out. I'm glad of the shin-pads as my leg bangs against the frame. 'You're such a skinny runt. You weigh less than my dog.'

I don't like the comparison. I stuff my feet in my shoes as fast I can. 'Can we just get out of here?'

'Good idea. You carry the stuff.' He thrusts the bag

and laptop back into my arms.

'Sure.'

Make the skinny runt do the work, why don't you?

He leads me around the side of the house. Then he freezes and backs up.

'What is it?' I ask.

'Shhhhhh,' he warns. 'The cops are here!'

'What do we do?'

'Follow me.' He pushes past, back through the gate and over the lawn. He clambers onto the fence.

'Dump the laptop. Give me your hand,' he urges. He hauls me up and we drop to the other side.

'POLICE! STOP RIGHT THERE!' We can hear the cops in the garden. They must have caught a glimpse of us as we went over.

'Move!' hisses Sammo, pushing me forward.

I sprint across the field in the darkness, the bag bouncing against my backside. I glance back. Sammo is right behind me. Behind him, I can see the silhouettes of two police officers climbing over the fence. They're giving chase.

It's only a matter of seconds before they're coming straight at us. One of them is shouting into their walkie-talkie, calling for backup. We can hear sirens in the distance.

'What now?' I pant.

For the first time, Sammo looks worried. 'You still want a coach, don't you?' he says. 'You want me to keep managing the Foxes?'

'Of course, why?'

'Well, in that case, play along. The most you'll get is a caution.'

'What?'

'If you tell on me, you'll regret it.'

My brain doesn't have time to work out what he's trying to say. Before I figure it out, Sammo rugby-tackles me. I land heavily and he climbs onto my back, pinning me to the ground, my face pressed in the mud.

'Don't worry, officers!' he shouts. 'I got him! I caught the thief! You can arrest him now!'

13. GUILTY

Sammo yanks me to my feet, a tight grip on my arm. I realise how guilty I look. He's stitched me up, good and proper.

I recognise Sergeant Brillin as he comes closer, puffing and panting. 'Well,' he says, shining a light in my face, 'if it isn't the orange burglar!'

Great, there is a nickname. And it sucks. Just when I thought it couldn't get any worse.

'I saw him breaking into that house,' says Sammo, 'and when I asked him what he was doing, he ran, so I gave chase. Thank goodness you guys got here when you did.'

I have to give it to him: he's a convincing liar.

'That was very neighbourly of you, sir.'

'It felt like the right thing to do.' Sammo's not just planning to come out of this innocent. He wants to be a hero.

'Wait a minute,' says the sergeant, peering at him. 'Aren't you the boy's coach?'

Sammo squirms a little. 'Yeah. I took over the team a

couple of weeks ago. That's why I was suspicious when I drove past and saw Jed out here in Welbeck wearing his Foxes kit. I knew we didn't have training tonight, and I remembered what you said about a kid dressed like that breaking into houses. I hung around to check what he was up to.'

'Well, it seems you caught him red-handed!' Sergeant Brillin holds out his hand for the bag. 'May I?'

I hand it over and he rifles through the contents.

'My, my, haven't you been busy?'

'I can explain–' I begin, but the sergeant cuts me off.

'Oh no, you don't. Not here. Not right now. We need to chat with you when your parents are around. Or another appropriate adult. Until then, you keep shtum. Understand?'

I nod. I no longer feel nervous. Now that the police are here, it's over. There's nothing to fear.

Except being taken to prison, of course.

'What happens now?' asks Sammo. 'You gonna charge him?'

'Possibly. Once we've had a chat with his parents and heard what he has to say.'

'I should warn you, officer,' says Sammo, 'when I caught him, he threatened me. He said if I didn't let him go, he was going to accuse me of being in on it too.'

'That's not–'

'What did I say, lad?' cuts in Sergeant Brillin. 'Not another word. You'll get your chance to tell us your side of the story.'

I wipe my muddy hands on my football shirt, then hold them out. 'Ok, sure. Are you gonna handcuff me or what?' I ask.

'There's no need for that. Not if you come quietly.' Sergeant Brillin turns to Sammo. 'I'm going to have to ask you to come to the station too, sir, if you don't mind. We need a full statement. I'm sure you understand.'

'I'd be happy to help,' says Sammo, with a charming smile.

***

We take a brief ride in the police car. Sammo is sitting next to me. Occasionally he glances over, a satisfied smirk on his face. He thinks he's gotten away with this.

But he's wrong.

There's something he doesn't know. When I was in his car earlier, I slipped Sergeant Brillin's business card into my shoe. I knew what I had to do.

In Tristan's house, I got the opportunity, and I took it. I called Sergeant Brillin and told him what was going on.

It wasn't an easy decision. I knew it would ruin my reputation when everyone found out I'd been thieving with Sammo. Worse still, we'd lose our coach and the Foxes would fold.

But Mr Hughes' words had stuck with me: *You have to decide what's right. Then do it. And if that gets you into trouble, so be it.*

So, Sergeant Brillin knows Sammo is guilty. I'd like to be there when they tell him. Sammo is going down. Of course, that's not to say I'm innocent. I expect they'll charge me as well. I probably deserve it.

My mum has no way of getting to Welbeck, so once they've dropped Sammo at the police station, we start back to Ferndale.

'Jed, you did a brave thing, calling us like that,' Sergeant Brillin reassures me. 'We can't chat properly until we get to your place, but don't worry. We'll soon get this all sewn up.'

His words give me hope. Maybe I'm not in as much trouble as I think.

'It's this one,' I say, a few minutes later, as we arrive at my house. I wish it wasn't, but there's no point lying.

'Righty Ho.'

We get out the car and Mum throws open the front door.

'Jed! What's been going on!'

'Don't worry, madam. As I explained on the phone, your son is helping us with our enquiries. No need to panic.'

Mum glances up the street, wondering what the neighbours will think. Then she shows the police officers into our crummy lounge.

'What's this about?' she demands.

'Your son has been involved in some thefts around the local area. But we believe he was forced into them.'

'Thefts? I thought you were at football practice,' she says, a hurt look in her eyes. 'You told me you had extra training.'

My stomach tightens with guilt. 'I did. Sort of. That's what Sammo told me.'

'If we could just ask Jed some questions, we'll soon sort this out,' assures Sergeant Brillin. 'Jed, all I need you to do is tell us the truth, ok?'

I nod.

'Well, that will make a pleasant change,' mutters mum. I realise that when the police have finished with me, I'm probably gonna be grounded for life.

The officers ask loads of questions and I tell them everything. It all comes pouring out.

'So, if I understand you correctly, Jed,' concludes

Sergeant Brillin, 'this all happened because you were so desperate for a coach?'

'It sounds stupid when you put it like that, but yeah, that's right.'

'You must be really committed to your team.'

'I am. I mean, I was. I'd do anything to keep it going. Well, *almost* anything.' I give the policeman an awkward smile and fiddle with the top of my football socks. 'Are you going to charge me? For the thefts?'

'No, I don't think so. You didn't plan any of this. The way I see it, you're a victim.'

'Really? Thanks.'

'If you don't mind me saying,' added the other officer. 'You still don't seem all that happy.'

'I am, but I'm not,' I admit. 'It's just that the Foxes are going to fold. There's no way Sammo will coach us now.'

'He wouldn't be allowed,' agrees the sergeant. 'Not after treating you like that.'

I knew that would be the case. Besides, I didn't want Sammo ordering us around, on or off the pitch. But I'm gutted that there's no-one else to do it. And I'm worried about something else: 'How will I tell the others?'

'When's your next training?' asks Sergeant Brillin. 'I mean *real* training, rather than breaking into people's houses.' He has a twinkle in his eye and I give a weak smile.

'Tomorrow. Half past four. At the field by the Bull pub.'

'Well, how about I come along and explain to your team what's been going on? I think that might help, don't you? Until then, I suggest you keep quiet.'

'Seriously? Would you?'

'Sure. It's the least I can do. Anyway, we'll be off now. We've got everything we need for the moment. And I'm looking forward to hearing what Sammo has to say for himself.'

Mum lets them out. As soon as they've gone, she turns to me. 'I can't believe this has happened, and you didn't tell me about it!'

'Sorry,' I mumble. 'I didn't want to stress you out. And we needed a coach. It all happened bit by bit.'

She sits on the coffee table and takes my hand in hers. 'You know you can always talk to me, Jed.'

'I know.' My eyes well up with tears; I wipe them with the back of my hand. 'I'm sorry, I really am.'

She moves over and hugs me. 'Ok, apology accepted. I think you've learned your lesson. I just need to know that there's nothing else you're hiding from me?'

I'm about to assure her I'm not, that she knows everything. Then I remember the paper round, and that I lied about my age on the form. I can't keep that from her any longer. Not now. Not after this.

'Well, there is one more thing…'

14. SURPRISE

Mum makes me quit.

I have to admit to the newsagent that I'm twelve. As I walk up to the counter, I wonder how angry he's going to be.

'No football kit this morning?' he says, surprised.

'I have to give up the paper round,' I mumble.

'Already?' he asks. 'I thought you needed the money?'

'I do, but...' I trail off.

'Well, come on, boy! Spit it out!'

'The thing is, I'm only twelve.'

He lets out a long sigh and places his hands on the counter. 'I always thought you were too young, but your mum signed the form!'

'I altered the date of birth,' I admit. 'I'm sorry.'

'Can't say I'm not disappointed,' he says. 'You were a good paper boy.'

I look up, surprised. 'Was I?'

'Not many kids turn up on wet and windy days and get the papers delivered. Not without mummy or daddy's help. That takes commitment. When you turn thirteen, you come and see me. We'll see if any rounds are available then, ok?'

'Deal.' I'm relieved that he's taken the news so well.

He roots around in the till and pulls out some cash. 'Here you go. This is what I owe you.'

'Thanks!'

It's good to have some money. I wonder if it will be enough for some new boots. I know it won't get me a decent pair, but right now I'll settle for anything without holes. Then I remember the Foxes are at an end, so it's hardly worth it.

***

Thursday after school.

I don't know whether to put my kit on for practice. If I don't, the others will know that something is wrong. It's easier to act normal and hope that Sergeant Brillin turns up like he promised.

Once I'm ready, I head out the house and wander down the street, kicking random stones aside. I might as well kick something; it's not going to be a football. Our plan to save the Foxes seems stupid now. It never worked, just got me in trouble.

Given my mood, I wish it was raining, but it's nice and sunny, perfect for a kickaround. When I get to the field, everyone seems cheerful. Sammo let us play football on Tuesday, so as far as they're concerned, everything is going well. Wait until they find out.

'You alright, Jed?' asks Dave. He can see I'm not happy.

'I guess.' I don't want to get into it.

It's not many minutes before a car pulls up, but not the police car I expect. Sergeant Brillin steps out of a small, blue hatchback, wearing a retro tracksuit.

'Afternoon, lads,' he says. 'Could you gather round?'

My teammates shuffle over, but aren't sure why he's here. I don't think many of them remember who he is without his uniform.

'I'm Sergeant Brillin,' he explains. 'You might remember we met when I asked you about the boy who'd been carrying out burglaries. Well, I've come with some news. I'm afraid that your coach, Sammo, has been arrested. It turns out he was behind the whole affair.'

'Seriously?' Dave sounds gutted. Everyone else is too shocked to speak.

'Yes, he's been fencing stolen goods for some time.'

'But he didn't even have an orange Foxes kit,' points out Miles, 'and you said it was a boy our age who did the thefts.'

Sergeant Brillin hesitates. He doesn't want to drop me in it. I decide to come clean and save him the hassle.

'That's because I did it,' I admit. 'Sammo made me break into houses for him when he was meant to be giving me extra training.' I expect they'll hate me now that they know what I've done.

But they appear more confused than angry. Only Rex is looking at the ground. It's his brother that we're talking about. I wonder if he's mad at me or ashamed of him. Probably both.

'Jed was the reason we caught Sammo in the end,' says Sergeant Brillin. 'He was brave enough to do the right thing and own up.'

'Good on you, Jed,' says Dave, putting his hand on my shoulder. 'That must have been a tough call.'

The others are nodding. They don't seem annoyed or disappointed.

'I couldn't do it anymore,' I say, my voice shaky, 'even though it meant we'd lose our coach.'

'I don't blame you, mate.' Brandon catches my eye. 'You did the right thing. I can't believe he made you do that!'

I realise I couldn't hope for better friends. We've always been a great team. Some sides play football: they train together and play at the weekends, but that's all they do. They're just football teams. The Foxes are a family. Even though we're still able to see each other, boy am I going to miss playing football with these lads.

'The plan failed,' I sniff, glancing at Dave. I feel that I've let him down.

'We did our best,' he shrugs. 'That's all we could do.'

'Well, lads,' says Sergeant Brillin, 'as it happens, I have a proposal for you that might be of interest.'

More confused glances. No-one has the faintest idea what he's talking about.

'You see,' carries on the sergeant, 'I only moved to this village recently. My lad, Luke, is your age, and he's looking for a team. When I saw you boys playing last Saturday, and heard from Jed how passionate you are, I thought it would be amazing if he could join the Foxes. What do you say?'

'We definitely need more players,' says Dave, 'but I'm afraid he'll need to find another team. We all will. Without Sammo, we don't have a coach.'

'Oh,' says Sergeant Brillin, 'did I forget to mention that I was offering to be your coach?'

My heart stops. Then starts again. I can't believe what I just heard. Neither can anyone else.

'Are you saying you'll coach us?' says Dave, a little stupidly. That is, after all, exactly what the sergeant said.

'Yes, lad. I'll coach the Foxes. If you'll have me?'

'Yes!' I shout. I have no idea if he knows anything about football, but he's a friendly adult who's willing to give it a go. How bad can it be?

'Sure!'

'Absolutely!'

'But don't you have to work?'

'I do flexible shifts,' he says. 'I often have to do nights so I get this time off. Besides, I figure it'll be easier to keep an eye on you troublemakers here on the pitch than it will to chase around the village after you.' He catches my eye and winks.

'We've got a coach!' shouts Dave, as the news sinks in.

'Wooohoooo!' The shouts become a wild celebration as we grab each other's shoulders and start jumping up and down.

'That's quite a welcome!' laughs the sergeant. 'Let me introduce you to Luke!'

He beckons to his car, and his son jumps out and runs over. The boy smiles shyly as he approaches.

'Hi Luke,' says Dave, 'welcome to the Foxes!'

'Thanks.'

'Before you get carried away,' says Sergeant Brillin, 'there are a few conditions to my offer.'

Everyone quietens down. We know what it's like to

have a coach who makes demands.

'First, I need to know that you're committed to the team, and that you'll give a hundred percent. No slacking off practices to play Nintendo or whatever.'

I grin, and so do the others.

Luke looks away, embarrassed. 'Dad,' he mutters, 'no-one plays Nintendo any more. It's Xbox or PS5.'

'Whatever,' says Sergeant Brillin. 'Everyone who wants to play, has to practice.'

'Agreed,' says Brandon. 'You won't have a problem with that. We always show up. It's that kind of team. And besides, none of us own a *Nintendo*!'

We all laugh.

'Ok, fair enough. My second condition is more important,' says the sergeant.

'Yeah, what's that?' asks Dave.

'That, boys, is that football is meant to be fun! If you're not having fun, there's no point playing. Ok?'

Now we're smiling again, relieved. This sounds a lot better than the harsh regime Sammo inflicted on us.

'Let's get started. Tonight, we'll have a game, and spend some time getting to know each other. Sound good?'

'Yeah!'

I notice even Rex has a smile on his face. Maybe he's

not as mad as I thought. As we take our positions on the field, I walk over and put my hand on his shoulder. 'Hey, Rex,' I say. 'I'm sorry about your brother. I didn't mean to get him into trouble.'

He looks at me with sad eyes. 'I know. They reckon he'll only get community service. It's probably for the best. He was going right off the rails. I tried to warn you guys.'

'You did.'

'It's not all bad, though,' admits Rex. 'My parents are on his case, so he can't bully me any more! And also, I got to move into the bigger room!' He smiles. 'I've been after that for ages. I finally get my own bathroom!'

'That's great!' I give him a high five.

'You want to know something else funny?' he says to me, a cheeky smile forming on his lips.

'Sure, what?'

'He's no longer allowed to drive, and my parents are making him pay people back for all the stuff he stole. Guess what was the only job he could get?'

I shake my head, clueless.

'Your paper round!' says Rex. 'The newsagent put an urgent advertisement up today after you quit, and my dad made Sammo apply.'

I laugh out loud. 'That's hilarious! He's gonna hate

that! It's an absolute mission going out to Briar's Farm!'

'He's not looking forward to the early mornings,' agrees Rex, 'but it serves him right!'

I don't think I could be any happier. It may only be a fun practice, but I play my heart out. The Foxes have survived!

When we take a break, I notice Dave, Rex and a couple of others having a whispered conversation. Rex is handing something over.

'Hey lads, what gives?' I ask, curious. It's not like them to keep secrets.

'Well,' says Dave, 'we've got some good news.'

'I don't know if I can handle any more good news tonight. I already think I'm dreaming.'

'Well, you won't be wanting this then,' he says, casually opening his hand to reveal a wad of notes.

'Wait, what is that?'

'It's money, Jed. It's the cash we paid Sammo on Tuesday. Rex's mum insisted we all got it back, so he brought it with him to practice. We've had a chat and, rather than split it back up, we want you to have it. Get yourself some new boots.'

I glance down at mine. I'm tempted, but I have principles. 'You know I'm not a charity case,' I say, a little half-heartedly. I could get a quality pair with that money.

'We know,' sighs Dave. 'But we figure you've earned this. Call it a finder's fee for getting us a new coach! That's going to save us all tons of money in the long run! And you can even pay us back, by scoring loads of goals!'

I give in.

'Deal,' I say. I take the money and count it.

It's all there. Sixty quid. I can't believe my luck.

The Foxes are special, that's for sure. We do everything we can for one another. We always have.

Even as I think that, I notice Luke is standing awkwardly by himself. He doesn't know any of us. That needs to change.

I jog over to introduce myself; it's time to make a new friend.

***

When my alarm goes off at 7am the next morning, I could roll over and go back to sleep.

It's tempting.

But one last time I pull on the neon Liverpool kit and make my way quietly down the stairs. I scribble a brief note for mum, then grab my bike and head to the paper shop.

You'd think it was the last place I wanted to go after the torture of the last few weeks of early mornings and freezing rain, and you'd be right. But there's something I have to see.

Sammo.

I want to see him pay for his crimes. I need to watch him suffer. Maybe that makes me a bad person, but it's how I feel. I'm still afraid of him, though. He can't know I'm here. I hang back, around the corner, safely out of sight.

Then, I wait.

A few minutes later, he turns up, a sullen scowl on his face as he skids his posh mountain bike to a halt outside the shop under a streetlamp. He was never a cheerful guy, but I've never seen him so miserable. He looks like he's chewing a lemon.

Better still, he's dressed in proper cycling gear, head to toe in neon lycra. In the drizzle, it looks more like a wetsuit. And I thought what I had to wear was bad! I wonder if it's part of his punishment, or if his mum made him wear it so he'd be safe. Either way, it's hilarious. I slip out my phone and sneak a photo. I know I shouldn't, but I can't resist.

I don't plan on sharing it with anyone. If Sammo finds out I even took that photo then I'm dead.

But I am gonna look at it.

Every. Single. Day.

I'm gonna smile as I think about him out here on dark, wet mornings, carrying that heavy bag of papers.

Over the harsh winter months, I'll know he's cycling for miles along the muddy track to Briar's farm while I snuggle under my duvet.

As I look at that photo, I'll know that it's worth doing the right thing, even when it's hard, and that crime doesn't pay in the end.

And, best of all, I'll know that Sammo got exactly what he deserved.

A NOTE FROM THE AUTHOR

Thanks for reading 'The Crafty Coach'.

I hope you enjoyed it, and you're looking forward to hearing more stories about Jed and the Ferndale Foxes.

I have at least two more exciting adventures due to be published soon: 'The Sneaky Sub' and 'The Terrible Tournament'. They're going to be full of action, suspense and... you guessed it... football!

Meanwhile, there are a few things you can do before you get them:

First, you can connect with my readers' club at:

www.subscribepage.com/footballkids

If you're under thirteen, your parents will need to sign up for you. I'll keep you informed of any new releases, as well as giving you opportunities to get freebies, prizes and giveaways. Best of all, there's the opportunity to send me football photos to try to win a place on one of my book covers!

Second, you can check out my Instagram account @zacmarksauthor where I post football forfeit challenges, where kids sometimes end up egged or with boots full of shaving foam! Check it out and get your parents to message me if you want a challenge of your own!

Finally, it would be a huge help to me if you would get your parents to post a review on Amazon for this book. Could you do that? I promise I read every review!

Stay connected – I love hearing from my readers, and who knows, maybe you or your team could make it into one of Jed's adventures!

Thanks so much for being a part of my story.

Zac.

ARE YOU A FOOTBALL STAR?

Are you a boy aged 9-13 who loves football?

Do you like having your photo taken?

Do you look good in football kit?

Interested in appearing on a book cover?

Or getting some free books?

Visit www.subscribepage.com/footballkids for information on all this and more!

COMING SOON

Don't miss out on Jed's next adventure: 'The Sneaky Sub'. Here's what it's about:

Strange things have been happening to Jed. Someone doesn't want him to play football, and they're giving him a hard time. Worse still: it's one of his teammates, but he doesn't know which.

Whoever it is, they're making his life a total misery. Would one of his friends really be that mean?

Jed has to solve the mystery, and fast! Whatever happens, he has to get back on the pitch. He can't allow himself to be defeated by the Sneaky Sub!

'The Sneaky Sub' is the next book in the 'Football Boys' series and will be released soon. To stay up to date, sign up to my readers' club at:

www.subscribepage.com/footballkids

Printed in Great Britain
by Amazon

71642571R00073